LIBRAM
MYSTERIUM

Libram Mysterium is published by Pulp Mill Press

Cover art and interior Illustrations by Christopher Conklin

First Edition
Published in 2014

ISBN: 978-0-9936324-0-2

Pulp Mill Press
www.pulpmillpress.blogspot.ca

LIBRAM MYSTERIUM

EDITED BY SEAN P. ROBSON

CONTENTS

MORDIGGIAN'S DUE

JOSH REYNOLDS

"They say that Mordiggian is a just god, who claims only the dead and has no concern for the living, save those who would violate his law and profane his temple," Amina Algol said, pricking Aramash's unshaven throat with the tip of her curved sabre even as she kicked the door to his room shut behind her. He blinked in surprise and his jaw sagged. She went on, "And then his wrath is all-consuming and relentless."

Dark, like all the folk of Khem, Amina was neither tall nor short, and she wore no helm or hood, so that her dark hair, tied in serpentine braids, spilled across her shoulders. She was clad in rattletrap gear—a banded cuirass scavenged from a battlefield and hastily repaired with bits and bobs of other armour, and stained travel-leathers made from zoog-hide. She had neither gloves nor boots, both to make for easy climbing and because she found such things uncomfortable and cumbersome.

Aramash, by contrast, was a Dreamer, and his origins ambiguous. He might have been from Meroe or Carcassonne or any one of a hundred places, and by his dress, might have been confused for a trader, if one did not notice the scars on his fingers and the muscles that bespoke hard graft. His face paled as her dark eyes met his and he swallowed thickly, trying to dredge up some form of vocal protest.

"But then, you knew that, did you not, Aramash?" Amina smiled, and, seeing his distress, answered for him. "That was why you fled Khem on a fast horse, and then Meroe, and after that Ulthar before finally finding your back against the Southern Sea, here in Dylath-Leen." Amina's smile faded. "You knew that Mordiggian would claim his due, one way or another. Where are they, Aramash?"

Aramash stumbled back, and Amina padded lightly after. The tip of her Khemish blade never left the ridge of his Adam's apple. The blade was a gift from her father, to make up for her lack of claws and fangs.

Her family had never made an issue of her deformity, though her brother Arif mocked her when he thought he could get away with it.

She had fed from her mother's teats, the same as her brothers and sisters, and learned how to pry open tombs and sarcophagi from her father. And it was her father who had given her the name 'Amina'—it meant 'charnel-blossom' in the meepery of the ghouls. She did not think the name suited her, for she was hardly a delicate flower, though she had never said so.

"Where are they, Aramash? If you do not find your tongue, I will bite off your fingers and eat them like candies," Amina said, lifting his chin with the flat of her blade. She grinned, showing off her teeth. She had filed some of them as a younger woman, to fit in. They ached sometimes, but the effect on the unprepared was worth it. Aramash grew even paler and began to stutter. Annoyed, she took in his lodgings at a glance.

It was the best room in a canal-front inn, meaning it stank of mould and rot, but showed no evident signs of either. The stink did not trouble her overmuch. Noisome scents were her birthright, and compared to some, the bouquet offered up by Dylath-Leen's recesses was as sweet as rose water. The room was empty, save for a lumpen mass that approximated a bed. Through the lone window, the shapes of the black basalt towers of Dylath-Leen rose over dark, uninviting streets.

"Charming," she murmured.

Aramash finally found his tongue. "What—what do you want?"

Amina made a face. "The canopic jars you stole from the temple of Mordiggian, Aramash. You haven't sold them yet, I trust, because if so..."

"No, no!" Aramash yelped, raising his hands. "I haven't!"

"Good. Where are they?"

"I—I can't give them to you," he said. "I promised them to a man."

Amina growled. It wasn't half as good as one of her siblings could manage, but it got the point across. Aramash's face went the colour of whey. "I can't!" he said again. "He'll kill me—no, worse than kill me."

"Who is he?"

Aramash hesitated. She growled again and he blurted, "N—Nosomo of Thul!"

Amina cocked her head. "Ha. Now there's the meat of it," she muttered. There was only one sort of person who'd buy something stolen from the house of the god of graveyards, and they were not the sort to be trifled with. "Nosomo the necromancer," she said. Aramash's head bobbed.

She frowned. Necromancers were a dirty business; something beyond the pale—a monstrous evil, whose presence no sane man could tolerate for long. For her folk, they fell somewhere between poachers and thieves, which was almost as bad. Nosomo was reputed to be one of the worst of a bad lot; he was rumoured to have learned the secrets of the Vaults of Zin, and made compact with Vulthoom in his red prison. If he was involved...She looked around the room again. There was no place to hide the jars, except...

"You've got a loose board," she said. Aramash's eyes flickered to the side, instinctively showing her what she wanted to know. It had been a bluff, but he was too nervous to realize that. She stepped back, extending her arm and pressing the tip of her blade hard to the hollow of his throat. "Pry it up," she said.

"He'll do things to me—I didn't know who he was, I thought he was just a collector—I can't..." he trailed off as he saw the look on her face.

"Mordiggian is a just god," she said, "But wrathful."

Aramash swallowed and stooped, prying at the board. As he worked, she said, "Where are you meeting him?"

"Here," he said hesitantly. "I thought you were him at first," he added, half-accusingly. "That's why I let you in..."

"Then you're blind as well as foolish," she said. He didn't reply. The board popped loose after a moment of wiggling and he reached down into the gap to retrieve a duo of shapes swaddled in sack-cloth.

"Careful," she said.

"I got them here from Khem didn't I," he spat, forgetting his fright for a moment.

"That you certainly did. Though I'm sure you've had cause to consider the wisdom of that little adventure since then. Uncover them," she said.

He did as she demanded and carefully peeled away the sack-cloth to reveal the two canopic jars, with their painted animal faces and identical torsos. She did not know who—or what—was in them. It did not matter. They belonged to the charnel god and she would see them returned.

"Wrap them back up, carefully, and give me whatever satchel you used to bring them here."

Aramash clutched the jars to his chest, and made as if to protest. Before a single word could slip his lips, however, the door thudded in its frame. They both looked at it, and then at one another. Aramash's jaw sagged and he whined, "He's early..."

"His bad luck," Amina said, stepping to the side of the door. "Let him in," she added, and then pressed a finger to her lips.

Aramash hesitated, but only for a moment. Whatever his other faults, the Dreamer wasn't slow-witted. He well knew what the price for violating the sanctity of Mordiggian's temple was, and he probably hoped to escape that fate while Amina dealt with the necromancer.

He wouldn't, of course. He had been marked, and they had his scent now. Wherever he went, however far he ran, they would catch him and crack his bones. But here and now, the necromancer was more important. She clutched her blade tightly, readying herself.

Aramash opened the door, the jars still clutched to his chest, and hurriedly staggered back as a tall, thin shape bent and sidled through the door. Beneath the heavy black cloak it wore, its proportions were all wrong. It was too thin and it stank of preservatives and mouldering spices. It wore a waxen mask beneath it voluminous cowl and its fingers were wrapped tight in yellowing bandages. It loomed over Aramash. With a negligent gesture, it tossed a heavy pouch of coin onto the floor, and gold coins spilled out. Then, as silent as a tomb, it extended its hand.

Aramash licked his lips, his eyes darting from the coins to the thing's hand. Amina elbowed the door shut and slid behind the newcomer, her blade raised. "Hello," she said. The thing span about, far more quickly than she'd expected. Nonetheless, she reacted instinctively. Her blade swept up, and she carved through the thing's waxen mask and sent it reeling.

As the two halves of the mask fell away, a mummified horror was revealed; a snarling, leathery visage, punctuated by two, burning beast-orbs. Amina had seen worse, but not of late. She ducked beneath a looping blow, and her blade caressed the dead thing's chest through its robes, releasing a spray of incense and dust rather than blood. It brought a fist down on her shoulder, dropping her to her knees in a burst of pain. The old dead thing was far stronger than it looked. She hurled herself aside as it groped for her. Aramash had risen and pressed himself to the back wall, the canopic jars held to his chest. The thing whirled as Amina avoided it, and reached for Aramash, who yowled in fright. Bandaged fingers fastened on the Dreamer's skull. Bone and flesh popped and tore with an unpleasant sound. As his body slid down the wall, his killer snatched up the jars and hurried for the door.

The mummy fled down the stairs, moving with awkward speed. Amina hurried after it, not sparing a glance for the ill-fated Aramash. She cursed herself as she took the rickety, damp-warped stairs three at a time. If it got outside, there would be no way she could keep up with the dead thing's lolloping gait. The dead travelled fast.

The common room of the inn was in an uproar. The mummy staggered through the room, upending tables and slinging patrons aside as it made for the door. She bounded up onto a table and jumped from it to the next, trying to get ahead of the thing. But to no avail. The mummy struck the entrance to the inn and tore the door off of its hinges. It staggered out into the street and began to run as if its feet were aflame, scattering the afternoon crowd that clogged the streets. Amina hurried after it, using her elbows and shoulders to carve a path through the crowd. As she ran, she fished around inside her cuirass, digging for the finger-bone whistle dangling around her neck. She blew the whistle as loudly as she could, as she pursued the mummy through the labyrinthine streets, racing along the perpetually damp stones with the surety of one who'd hunted sweetmeats in tombs slimier than any back-street. But she could not keep up with her quarry, and she was fast growing tired. Her muscles burned with effort and her breath rasped in her lungs. It was all she could do to keep sight of the thing's flapping robes.

Then she caught the rasp of her siblings' paw-pads behind her and felt a flicker of relief. They had been waiting nearby, in hiding, so as not to unduly disturb the folk of Dylath-Leen. Ghouls were not unknown in the city, for there were many ghouls in the Dreamlands, for wherever man went, ghouls soon followed. Sometimes out of curiosity, but mostly for other, more material reasons. And it was for those reasons that many failed to find comfort in the presence of children of Mordiggian.

Her siblings had accompanied her from Khem, as was proper.

Ghouls travelled in packs, especially when hunting. The Dreamlands were dangerous, even for the eaters of the dead.

The two heavy shapes shouldered past her and bounded in pursuit. They knew what needed doing. They could smell the miasma of necromancy that followed their quarry better than she. Her siblings were hairy where mould didn't crust their piebald flesh, and had lolling doggy jaws set into their sloped skulls. They moved low to the street like hyenas, their heavy forelimbs hauling them along with rapidity as their cloven back legs propelled them forward. One struck a drover's cart and bounded onto the wall of a building. It ran across the surface of the wall for a moment, like a giant spider, before vaulting across the street to the buildings on the other side. The first fell back at her wordless exclamation and Amina caught up with it. She snagged a hank of her greasy hair and hauled herself onto her sister's broad, rubbery back as she put on a burst of speed. "Well met, Bera," Amina meeped.

"Well met, Amina," her sister growled. She glanced back at Amina and the setting sun caught on the ring of gold set into one delicate nostril. "Never fear; Arif will catch him. No dead thing has ever yet outrun him."

"Arif can't handle that thing on his own. It was raised by necromancy. Besides which, I only want him to harry it. I want to find out where it's going!" Amina said urgently. Bera growled in understanding.

"It will lead us to the necromancer," she said, "Clever, sister."

Arif had pulled far ahead of them, bounding from building to building with simian agility. As the caught up with him, their quarry burst from the tangle of streets into a plaza crowded with merchant's stalls and street-vendors. The smells of foreign spices, strange foods and tightly-packed humanity mingled into a pervasive miasma.

The mummy burst through the crowd without slowing. Men and women were trod upon or swatted aside, and the crowd began to churn and splinter as the realization that something untoward was occurring filtered through its collective consciousness. Arif struck a water-spout and vaulted into the air. The ghoul struck like a pouncing ape, bearing the mummy off of its feet. The two rolled across the cobbles, Arif's growls punctuated by the scrape of the mummy's robes and wrappings against stone. Then, suddenly, the mummy bobbed to its feet with what might have been the remnant of a warrior's grace, and backhanded the slavering ghoul, sending him flying into a fruit-seller's stall. The tent collapsed in on the squawking merchant and the yelping ghoul. The mummy paused for a moment, as if to survey the scene. Then, in a flare of ragged robes, it was gone.

Amina and Bera could not pursue it. The crowd bobbed and squawked, and the sight of a woman on the back of a ghoul did not help matters. People fled in all directions, yelling and screaming. Bera snapped at a few who got too close as Amina slid off of her back and hurried towards the thrashing shape struggling with the fruit-seller's tent. With a careful swipe of her blade, she slashed a hole in the tent and a blunt head poked out, eyes blinking.

"Did I get him?" Arif meeped as he pried himself out of the tent.

"Oh yes, and then he turned into a flock of crows and flew down my gullet," Bera growled.

"He did?" Arif looked around, wide-eyed.

"No, greedy-guts, he knocked you a-tumble and got away!"

"Good, it smelled bad," Arif meeped. He clawed at his snout for emphasis.

"No worse than any burial chamber and you've rolled in those often enough, brother," Amina said, smiling slightly. The crowd had thinned out. There had been stranger sights in Dylath-Leen, and even the fruit-seller wasn't squawking overmuch. Arif's teeth were even bigger than Bera's and he was uglier to boot.

"It does smell worse," the ghoul protested. He straightened. "I smell like shit."

"How is that any different than any other time?" Bera hissed, exposing her curving fangs at her brother. "Stop complaining!" She looked at her sister. "Well, Amina? Where do we go now?"

"We follow our noses," Amina said, tapping her own. "As he so eloquently put it, mummies stink worse than Arif."

Arif bristled at the teasing and grumbled unhappily. "Why are we bothering with this anyway, eh? What's one more or less necromancer?" he grunted. "What does the matter have to do with us?"

It had everything to do with them, of course, and Arif well knew it for all his complaints. They had a duty to the god and to their folk, who were the guardians of Mordiggian's halls. What had been stolen would be returned, and those who had stolen it would pay the price.

"Go home then, if that's how you feel. You know the way," Amina said, letting an edge creep into her voice. She loved her brother dearly, but he was, and always had been a lazy creature. Effort—the merest hint of effort, even—pained him as surely as fire or steel. "But we have a duty, and I, at least, intend to fulfil it."

"We will honour Mordiggian, sister, and he will have his due," Bera said, glaring at Arif, who quailed in mock-fear. "Arif is simply being petulant, as always." She snapped her jaws at their brother and he yelped.

"Can you follow its scent," Amina said, snapping her fingers to catch his attention.

"It stinks," Arif barked. Amina grabbed his snout and swatted him between the ears with the flat of her sword.

"Stop whining and pick up the scent, brother. You have the best nose this side of the Vale of Pnath," she said. "Find that mummy!"

Arif growled sullenly and sank into a crouch. His pink-tinged nostrils flared and then he was off, his snout perpendicular to the cobbles. Amina shared a look with Bera and then vaulted onto her sister's back once again. They loped after Arif.

The mummy had left a definite trail—bits of bandage and incense and dust marked its path. As fast as it had been moving, and as carelessly, that came as no surprise. The trail led them to the docks, where the sheer number of strange vessels momentarily unbalanced the trio.

Amina, perched on her sister's back, was struck dumb for several seconds. Never before in her life had she seen so many ships and of so many different designs, bearing so many different flags. A hundred nations were represented in the great stone quays of Dylath-Leen and men of those nations and more, including some that didn't actually exist, flocked to the city.

As the sun sank below the horizon, casting an orange wash across the dark waters and across the vessels in dock, Arif gave a bark and loped to the edge of a quay. "I think I found it," he said, pointing.

Amina followed the gesture and saw a black sailed, low-hulled galley of the kind used by the men of Sarkomand slowly slipping towards the outer quays. "I think we've arrived just in time," she said. "We need to get on that ship."

"How do we even know it's the right one?" Bera said doubtfully as she glared balefully at the water. Ghouls were strong swimmers, though they did not, as a rule, enjoy the water. Still, a strong stroke was useful when retrieving a water-logged corpse.

"Offhand, I'd say it's because it's sailing without benefit of oars or a favourable wind," Amina said, stripping off her armour and flinging it aside. "Ready for a swim, Arif?" she said.

Arif growled irritably, but trotted towards the edge of the quay. Bera joined him. The two ghouls looked at each other doubtfully. Amina snorted and dove in. The cold water was like a shock to her system and her teeth immediately began to chatter as she drove towards the galley. She heard a tremendous splash behind her as her siblings followed suit.

She had learned to swim in the warm, turgid rivers of Khem, where you only had to be faster than a few over-fed crocodiles. But catching a moving galley was another matter. She wouldn't even have contemplated such an attempt, had she not feared that they would lose the galley in the Southern Sea. Her muscles burned with exertion, but she ignored the pain and kept swimming. Her siblings paddled beside her, keeping pace, their yellow gazes locked on the galley. "It's not moving very fast," Arif burbled, snorting water out of his nose as he paddled.

"Thank the gods," Amina muttered. Neither of her siblings seemed the least fatigued; yet another reminder of her deficiencies. Arif glanced at her and, as if knowing what she was thinking, he ducked beneath her so that she slid onto his back.

"Hold on to me," he said gruffly, "You're too slow."

Amina gratefully did just that, smiling slightly. "Thank you, brother."

"You're ugly, too," he retorted.

Before she could think of a reply, Arif reached out a long arm and sank his claws into the aft hull of the ship. Bera was already scrambling up and as Arif followed suit, she reached down to grab Amina's hand. "Up sister," she said.

Amina vaulted upwards over the rail of the galley and as one, two dozen dead men turned to look at her. She froze, fingers pressed to the hilt of her blade. The men were newly dead; she could tell as much from the smell as from the state of them. Broken necks and burst bellies were the most obvious signs of dispatch. They started towards her, blind eyes staring, hands reaching. Behind her, Bera and Arif huffed and grunted as they hauled themselves over the rail to join her.

"Necromancers," Bera chuffed, "No subtlety."

"They don't need subtlety when they've got walking corpses," Amina said as she drew her blade. She didn't see the mummy anywhere. Her eyes found the captain's cabin at the fore of the galley. There was a strange light flickering behind the windows. "We need to get through them."

"Ha, this part I like," Arif said, jaws set in a doggy grin. His claws gouged the deck and he inhaled deeply. "They smell...delicious." Bera grunted agreement and the two ghouls sprang forward. They crashed into the dead like twin thunderbolts. The zombies were numerous, but that simply added to the fun for Amina's siblings. As they romped through the dead, they opened a path, and Amina darted towards the cabin. She hit the door with her shoulder and it sprang open, sending her sprawling. She rolled aside as a dried, withered foot slammed down mere inches from her head.

The mummy had divested itself of its robes, and wore only a tattered loincloth and a wide, heavy-looking bronze torc, gone green from verdigris. She could just make out the faint spider-webs of faded tattoos curling across its leather flesh and the weird shape of the star-sign of ancient Mnar beneath the verdigris on the torc. As it raised its foot to stomp again, she pushed herself to her feet. Her sword sang out and the mummy jerked back as she carved a chunk from its shrunken belly.

She looked around, searching for its controller. He wasn't hard to spot. The necromancer was of no race of men she was familiar with, but she recognized him as the man the late, unlamented Aramash had feared easily enough regardless. His face had been painted to look like a skull and he wore ratty furs over stifling robes that were stiff with the effluvium of the necropolis, and bracers made from the flayed and dried faces of men. The skulls of rats, cats, zoogs and other small creatures dangled from around his neck and he wore iron rings on his fingers. He sat in a circle of smouldering braziers, chanting slowly and weaving his fingers in complicated gestures that resembled the movements of a leaf caught in a high wind. He was obviously moving the galley with a conjured wind. Beside him sat the canopic jars.

"Nosomo, I presume," she said.

"Who are you to speak the name of Nosomo of Thul so blithely," Nosomo rasped. His urine-coloured eyes narrowed and he smiled suddenly, displaying blackened teeth. "Never mind; I shall learn all of your secrets directly. Kill her, Ousigos!" he screeched. "Bring me her scalp for my belt!"

Ousigos moved to do as he was bid. Arthritic looking claws snapped towards her, impossibly fast. She ducked and scrambled aside. She struck at him again, and the mummy swatted aside the blow. "You cannot defeat him," the necromancer cackled. "Ousigos was the greatest wrestler of sunken Sarnath in life, and in death he is even greater still."

"Is he greater than Mordiggian?" Amina barked. Nosomo blanched, but recovered with a sneer.

"If he is not, then I certainly am!" he yowled. "I am a true master of death—moreso than any old god of Khem!"

The mummy lunged for her. One palm slapped against her blade and its fingers closed. With a jerk, it was yanked from her grip. She followed it, grabbing the hilt even as she rammed her elbow into Ousigos' throat. The mummy jerked back, as if it had been hurt. The necromancer's eyes widened slightly as the mummy's fingers brushed the torc and then jerked back as if they'd been burnt. Her blade reclaimed, Amina danced back, towards the door and Ousigos followed. He was strong—far stronger, even than her siblings, and tougher than any lump of ambulatory jerky had any right to be. Her eyes were drawn to the torc and, at a whim she jabbed at it, twisting between Ousigos' grasping hands. The tip of her blade glanced off of the torc and Ousigos jerked again and his fleshless jaws gaped in a soundless snarl. His eyes blazed in something that might have been...hope? Her eyes narrowed.

"Kill her Ousigos," Nosomo said, rising to his feet, the jars in his hands. "I have summoned a wind to carry us safely from these waters with our prize. Kill her and I shall raise her and make her dance for you, as women once did in fair, cursed Sarnath!"

That did not seem to please Ousigos, from what she could tell, but he attacked again regardless. Amina, with instinct born of experience, focused on the torc. It was not of one piece, but was held about

Ousigos' neck by a bronze clasp. The dead could be bound by any number of means. But something as old as the mummy appeared to be required powerful bindings indeed, and no symbol was more potent in the Dreamlands than the star-sign of Mnar. The thought, when it came, quickly crystallized into deed as Ousigos' arms looped around her, and she allowed the mummy to jerk her forward. Her blade slid up quickly, sliding between the torc and the mummy's chest. With a burst of strength, she twisted back, out of the mummy's grip, and dragged the sword back, ripping the torc free from the mummy's neck with a screech of popping metal.

Ousigos let loose of her immediately, letting her topple to the floor. He turned slowly, beast-eyes blazing. Nosomo had ceased chanting now, and his face grew pale. "What," he said.

"Whoops," Amina said, lifting her sword to show him the torc hanging from it. The unbound dead were more dangerous than the other variety, especially to those who had enslaved them. "Mordiggian is a forgiving god. But Ousigos, I fear, is a different matter."

"No!" Nosomo howled. Ousigos lunged, long arms reaching, and the necromancer stumbled back, flinging up his hands. The canopic jars span from his grip and Amina scrambled to catch them. Ousigos snatched up Nosomo and swung him about in a grisly gavotte, knocking over the burning braziers in his fury. Fiery coals scattered across the cabin, and some struck Nosomo's filthy furs. Flames caught and spread hungrily as the necromancer screamed and writhed in Ousigos' grip. The smoke filling the cabin seemed to hunch and crouch like a waiting beast and Amina felt a thrill of fear as some vast shape seemed to uncoil within it. Ousigos wasn't the only one looking to take a bit of Nosomo's hide. Mordiggian's wrath had been invoked, and it was as inexorable as the creeping fire.

Amina didn't wait to see what would become of either the mummy or his former master. Holding the canopic jars and her sword, she hurried out of the cabin. She caught sight of her siblings herding the remainder of the corpses towards the mast. Body-parts littered the forecastle and limbless torsos wriggled across the deck, champing their jaws mindlessly. "Time to go," she shouted, as her siblings turned, "Stop playing with your food!"

"Back in the water, you mean?" Arif whined, backhanding a bo'sun.

"But we just got on the boat! And there're all these corpses..."

"The boat is on fire!" Amina said, sprinting past them.

"Good reason to get back in the water," Bera said, removing her jaws from the skull of a twitching zombie. She tossed the corpse aside and bounded after her sister. Arif grunted and followed after only a moment's hesitation, his greed warring with his common sense.

The water was just as cold as the first time around. As they swam back towards the inviting quays of Dylath-Leen, Amina paused and turned to see the ship drifting into the setting sun. As she watched, something tall and impossibly thin stepped out onto the deck in a plume of fire and smoke. It held something dull with verdigris in one claw-like hand as it swiftly stepped to the rail and vanished over the side. Of Nosomo, there was no sign.

The smoke rose above the burning vessel and twisted and coiled, becoming a blotch of darkness that seemed to draw in the light of the creeping flames and the sun both. The blotch briefly took the semblance of some daemonic giant and Amina fancied she saw a tiny shape, struggling in its clutches. And then, leaping and spreading up into the darkening sky, it was gone.

Ousigos had claimed his due. And Mordiggian had claimed his.

"Sister," Bera called.

Shivering slightly, Amina swam on.

JOURNEY TO THE INFINAT
JOSHUA GRABOFF

Olomeryn was always uncomfortable in Nibenlibe's house. That he was her archrival was known all throughout Ugram, but elves do not take umbrage at dining with their foes. Nibenlibe was handsome enough in his way. He was lissome and languid, his flesh a pale blue-white that was aswirl with prickly tattoos. He was smiling, which Olomeryn found irksome. His lithe body was draped across a mound of pillows and his tunic was a silvery sheer. His fingers glimmered with rings. Olomeryn knew that each one was the symbol of a long-lasting pact with ancient powers and she bridled at the way they flashed when he moved his hands, each more obscenely arcane than the last.

"My dear," Nibenlibe said casually, "it is inevitable that he will eventually lose interest in you." They were speaking, of course, of Argonal, Olomeryn's lover. "After all, no human can truly comprehend the intricacies of elvish courtship. For example, does he know that just last century you had a penis?"

Olomeryn bared her teeth in a parody of a smile. "Even the dullest human knows that we may change genders, when the mood takes us. After all, what else is magic for?" She twirled her own rings, reminding Nibenlibe with that subtle gesture that she too had many fiends at her command.

"Indeed, but the knowledge that our people as a whole sometimes change their shapes is much different from imagining your woman's vulva inverti—" Olomeryn choked on her wine, and Nibenlibe smiled broadly.

That was a point in his favor, for she had publicly shown her displeasure. She fought to control her anger.

She regained her composure and smoothed down her sandsilk gown. Her fingers curled around her goblet, but she made certain to hold it lightly, so that Nibenlibe would not claim victory from the tension in her knuckles. She leaned forward and conspiratorially said, "You know, he is a wizard. He is more used to dealing with things that men might find strange."

"Ah yes, he certainly might find something unpleasant joyful," Nibenlibe remarked triumphantly. "After all, they deal with such unpleasant things! It is our finest triumph that we no longer need to strain to achieve our mastery over magic." Olomeryn silently cursed herself for giving him the opening. "And we have no need of such things as the Infinat." Olomeryn started.

"The Infinat?" asked Olomeryn with a sly grin. Nibenlibe had made a terrible mistake. She could barely contain her venomous glee. Such names, names of ancient artifacts, devils, and demons alike were kept as highly guarded secrets. The fool had tipped his hand!

"Ah," he said nervously, and she silently crowed again, for his nerves showed on his face. "I thought you knew of it," he mumbled. To see him uncomposed was such bliss! He twitched to find a more comfortable position on his pile of cushions, the light of the crystalline lamps playing over his face.. Olomeryn could not have been more happy if he had been squirming. "Well, no matter," he said, trying to dismiss the foul-up.

But Olomeryn would not allow him that pleasure. "No, no," she said, feigning deep interest. "I am rapt. Tell me of this Infinat."

For a moment, Nibenlibe stared at her. Olomeryn first thought he would lie, but then she became certain that he would not; he would tell the truth, hoping that she suspected it was a lie and thus would be led astray. She leaned imperceptibly forward as he went on. "It is an archway," he grumbled. His voice was heavy with defeat and he needed to take a deep sip of wine from his cup before he went on. "A huge iron archway in the Desert of Horx. Its location is known only to a few—not me!" he said, preempting her question.

"Where does this Infinat lead?" she asked.

He could have said anything, or claimed ignorance. But she knew he wouldn't, for she had read his face for centuries and she could tell when he was going to lie. He knew as well, and she nodded as this understanding passed between them. "It leads to a library. A library on Flux."

Flux, the Golden Moon! "A hidden library?" she asked.

"Yes," he said. Olomeryn was disappointed. The victory felt hollow, for it was so easy. The scathing hedge of rivalry had fallen by the wayside and Nibenlibe was telling her simple truths now. She was on the verge of telling him to stop, of dismissing the entire conversation, but then she remembered Argonal. She felt a strange empathy for him, and knew that he would want to know of this hidden library. There was a stirring in her breast that she had not felt for longer than she could remember; she cared to help Argonal, for he was bold and young and brash. So she let Nibenlibe go on.

"Long ago some sorcerous creatures constructed a library on Flux to keep it safe from prying eyes. They knew that traveling there would be painful, for when was going to any of our five horrific moons easy? So, they made a key for the Infinat, an artifact which predated even them. The library contains endless knowledge; some say the Index of Fiends, which names every fiendish creature in creation." Nibenlibe sighed. "What's more, it is of interest to men, who love to learn things from demons and devils. For you see, this library, which was called Ratha, now lies close to the Cosmic Devoid."

Olomeryn refused to display ignorance in front of her rival. She knew the Cosmic Devoid of course, that horrific black sun that stood like a harbinger of the end days of Zaan. Someday, within the next century perhaps, the Cosmic Devoid would yawn wide and the Orbidium would shatter. The realms of Zaan were already stretched thin like taffy. Nibenlibe must have seen that she did not understand the implication. "One millennium in the library of Ratha is one day on Zaan. For you see, its proximity to the Devoid makes it so. Time stretches infinitely thin."

Olomeryn shivered gently. Argonal could go to Ratha, she thought, and when he returned he would be the most powerful archmage in our generation. She felt warm and joyful at that thought. And he will be happy, she added. The fact that this pleased her confused her ancient and jaded sensibilities, but she embraced it. She actually cared for the human boy.

***

Habernath was a minor devil. The learned arcanologists of faded Zaan had classified his kind as a 'scutling,' a being fit only for the most menial of tasks. Argonal shooed the little winged devil away as it tried repeatedly to shit onto his dinner. He sat on a terrace in Ugram, the sleek purple protrusion of marble jutting from Olomeryn's mansion to look out over the vast fields ruled by the elves. Overhead, the sky was a deep blue-black, the miniscule white ball of the sun puffing across it, alone in the yawning void. Every few seconds, Habernath would scoot his tiny bulging stomach back across the table towards Argonal's food and the wizard would absently brush the creature to the far side of the glistening stone surface.

"Habernath," he said warningly. The creature bore some resemblance to a homunculus, though its flesh was livid red instead of pale gray. It had a distended stomach and declined to wear any clothes to cover its miniature devilish member. A thicket of purplish hair grew to cover its crotch and armpits, but its head was completely bald. It giggled obscenely and rubbed its stomach.

"But master," it pleaded. "I feel so feculent!"

Argonal gave his devil a withering look. "You have no need to expel anything," he said angrily. "You never eat. It is not in your nature."

The wizard felt listless. The elves were fond of lethargic and byzantine games of wordplay that were beginning to tire Argonal. Each night when the dying sun set and the darkness of the Cosmic Devoid danced across the sky, garlanded in the Five Moons, the elves would issue forth from their palatial manors. Magical palanquins followed by crystal lamps hovered above the streets bringing pools of light through the dim and uninhabited lanes. Living with the elves was a lonely business. Argonal was used to the lively throng of the Magician's City where every street corner concealed beggars, thieves, and murderers.

Ugram was three or four times the size of Albor but while the Magician's City was alive with hundreds of thousands of people, there were no more than one thousand elves in all the marble tombs of Ugram. Argonal was deathly tired of schemes and plots and the passive aggression of the elves. They faced daily life with a sleepy lugubriousness; they stared into the Cosmic Devoid and knew that the Orbidium would come to a violent end within their own lifetimes, and they simply did not care.

If it was not for Olomeryn, he would have left long ago. She had taught him many magical secrets, and that had been the basis of their bond, but it had grown into something more. He felt something in her, something not as alien and dead as what he saw in the rest of her kind. Still, he could not stay in Ugram forever. Habernath was a constant reminder of what his true mission was: to learn: to learn enough magic, to understand the great pylons of the dwarves, maybe to succor this plane and keep it from dying, or barring that to escape. To escape the death of Zaan!

He heard the telltale tinkling that announced Olomeryn's return. He snorted a derisive laugh. Elves were so inundated with magic, so wealthy with its wonder that they could afford to enchant everything around them. Their fields tended themselves, their homes were kept tidy by retinues of invisible spirits, their lights burned with a strange crystalline glow that told of the enchantments kept within. There were magicians in Albor who would kill without hesitation to learn the mastery of any single one of these powers.

Olomeryn emerged onto the balcony, all smiles. Argonal wondered what she could be hiding, for the elves seldom smiled unless they had committed some treachery. She stood beneath a pair of fluted columns, her fleshy pale form hidden beneath her sandsilk gown. Her hair was silver and her eyes purple, and her hands worked behind her back. "What do you have there?" Argonal asked wearily. Undoubtedly it was something with which she could seek the upper hand in her eternal war against the magician Nibenlibe.

"Something for you," Olomeryn said coyly. Argonal waited for her to continue for he was irritated with her games. She took a few eager steps forward and whispered, "Have you ever heard of the Library of Ratha?"

Argonal hated the way she whispered these secrets, as though there were intruders listening. They both knew that Olomeryn's house was surrounded by threefold magical charms and a host of protective spirits that would never allow a word said on balcony or terrace, in hall or chamber, to be overheard by a spy. But his anger faded as he realized that she was talking about Ratha. He surged to his feet and clasped her by the arms. "Ratha?" he hissed, his own voice low. "Races have been exterminated in its pursuit! What did you find?"

She smiled demurely and produced a finely wrought iron-link chain. Dangling from it was a green pendant of emerald upon which the word Ratha had been etched. "I found this in Nibenlibe's manor," she said in a whispery giggle. "I would never have noticed it, but he had just this afternoon let slip the secret of journeying there. The necklace was left in full display! I had only to dispel his poisonous cantrips and pluck it for myself on my way out!"

Argonal drew her close and kissed her. The Library of Ratha! He could learn the secrets of the archmages, study deep and potent magics; unlike the ancients, he would not leave Zaan for some other plane, he would return from the hidden library and set everything right. He could save Zaan! He kissed Olomeryn again, deeper this time, and when they drew apart her pale flesh was flushed. She murmured, "Let me tell you of the Infinat."

***

The Desert of Horx was many miles south of Ugram, but Olomeryn had provided her lover with a magical bracelet inscribed with the names of three princely demons, each one lending an aspect of its power. Though Argonal still had to travel for days beyond the city, the bracelet ensured that he never wanted for food or drink; he never felt thirsty, never hungry, for the magic in the armband was such that it would sustain his body indefinitely. Habernath hated this and had taken to perching on Argonal's shoulder and chirruping unpleasantly in his ear.

They had been in the desert for two days, wandering through the sands, passing great stains of rust red along their way. Argonal supposed they were the remains of the massive iron idols the serpent men were said to have raised long ago, before they became stupid and slow in Zaan's dying hour. He closed his ears to Habernath's confounding noises and stopped for a moment to look at the sky.

The livid white sun was setting. The Devoid was huge on the horizon, the Five Moons dancing about it in their entropic circle. There was Mara, the Red Moon, whose influence governed the tides of passion and thus bloodshed. Below her was Ephrais, the Blue Moon, which controlled the tidal forces of magic. Next to Ephrais was Ceren the Green Moon, which commanded the growth of plants and animals. Above Ceren hovered Hurn, the Purple Moon, which drew veils and made secrets. Lastly, at the apex of the pentagon of dying moons, was Flux the Golden Moon, which had mastery over luck and fortune. And it is to Flux I go, Argonal thought.

As he stared, he realized that Habernath had stopped making noises. There was a haunting melody drifting across the dunes which set the wizard's teeth on edge. He scanned the horizon, trying to pinpoint it, but one of the desert's effects was to confuse all sound, sending it careening off distant sand and back again. At last he saw a smudge of stone against the dark sky. "There," he muttered to his devil. "Those rocks. What could be making that noise?" he asked.

"Skeletons keening, master," Habernath said, making a horrific sniffling and sucking sound in his nose.

"I think you're right, Habernath," Argonal agreed. He shifted his course towards the source of the sound and began to speed up. "And wild skeletons sing when they've found meat." Habernath burbled some kind of agreement, but Argonal didn't hear it. He was already reaching deep into his gut to prepare a spell. As the devil stretched to find a comfortable position to lounge in atop Argonal's shoulder, the wizard released the first syllables of his magic. They thundered from his stomach like mystic vomit, and suddenly his feet were skidding across the sand and the wind was whipping through his hair. Margon's Fleet Foot had taken hold of his boots, and his legs pumped at unseemly speeds.

He arrived in time to see the soulfully moaning skeletons circling a figure with its back against an upthrust red stone. From his dress and mannerisms, Argonal deduced he was a desert hermit. There were a few of those strange men dwelling out in Horx for reasons no one could discern. Some of them worshipped Gargonath the Grudgingly Good, but most were simply too mad to dwell in the semi-civilized towns of men.

The skeletons had made a semi-circle around him. Their haunting music echoed through the empty desert. Argonal said quietly to Habernath, "You will distract them!"

Habernath took wing, fluttering above Argonal's head. "I will not, master!" he piped. "They will rip me to shreds and feast upon me!"

The wizard's blunt features darkened. "Habernath," he said with an angry note in his voice, "You will do as I say or I will dismiss you from my service. You will be thrust out of Zaan in a most unpleasant manner and barred from all mortal realms. Do you want to spend the next thousand years as some devil-prince's butler?" The little creature's face fell.

"I will do as you say, master," Habernath whined. Argonal nodded and the devil struck off towards the skeletons.

While Habernath flew towards them, Argonal prepared Thyren's Horrific Shattering, forcing the words to flaming life in his gullet. His bile began to rise as it was displaced by the whirling forces contained within him. He advanced a few more meters, the Fleet Foot having faded into the desert night. The skeletons had turned upon Habernath, as the hermit was no challenge to them. The little devil was doing his best to tear at their limbs, but so far had only managed to anger them.

Argonal moved into range of the killing spell, his stomach boiling with force. Explosive words rang from his lips and the spell convulsed into being; Habernath clasped his ears and fell to the ground as the skeletons shrieked a death cry. Dust and sand were urged into frantic eddying whirlpools. The force of the spell rent the bones of the gathered skeletons to flinders, osseous chips flying in all directions. Habernath covered his head with his hands and screamed in fear. Argonal could feel his belly emptying, the burning fires of magic pouring out of his lips and into the world. When the spell had been cast he felt as though he had expelled some vital thing within him.

He staggered over to the hermit and held out a hand to help him stand. "You were lucky, old man," he sighed. It was then that he saw the man was no man at all—she was a pockmarked and goblin-faced woman, whose huge bulbous nose and beady eyes at once peered up at him from beneath the hood of ragged cloth she wore.

"You may call me Oka," she said in a voice like glass being drawn across slate. "Oka of the Red Spires. Thank you, traveler."

"As for me," said the magician, somewhat troubled by her appearance, "I am Argonal of Albor."

The old woman cooed in delight and clapped her hands with glee. "A wizard!" she said, "A sorcerer! And look, your familiar comes." She referred, of course, to Habernath, who was ambling over the dark sands towards them. His tone was low and his voice mumbled a bevy of curses, most of them directed at the sense of his master. His face had been bruised by the graceless slap and thunder of Argonal's shattering spell.

The wizard nodded. "Some might call me that," he said mildly, "though I am but a humble student of the art."

"Yes," the crone agreed, "your creature is rather puny and noisome, I see." Habernath was spitting gobs of phlegmy substance as he walked, leaving miniature pools of snotty filth simmering on the sand. "But come, we must eat. Night is almost upon us and the unblinking eye of the Devoid rises."

***

The crone Oka lived in a crook between two massive spires of red rock that stretched from the desert floor like the fingers of a maimed hand. She burned a fire beneath a huge iron cauldron within which desert mammals were stewing, meat on bone. Argonal had taken a seat opposite her, perched some ways up a slope of tumbled rock, while Habernath was warming himself perilously near to the blaze. He smiled lasciviously at his master, licking his thick worm-like lips.

"What brings you so deep into the desert?" Oka asked, stirring the thickening stew.

"Rumor," said the mage vaguely. He was hesitant to reveal his quest. Wizards are ever stingy with knowledge, for it is their one advantage against the world. Argonal was no different in that, and if life amongst the elves had taught him anything it was to be even more tight-lipped.

"Rumor?" asked Oka, repeating the word. She made chewing motions, as if tasting the concept in her cavernous mouth. "Rumor of what, master wizard?" she asked. "I have lived long here, and it may be that I know of what you seek."

"You would not know," Argonal responded haughtily, and he turned to look at the distant spray of the stars. The motion shifted his tunic and caused the iron necklace he wore beneath it to become momentarily visible.

Oka let out a knowing breath. "Ah-h-h-h," she said, "A key necklace!"

Argonal started as though the crone had seen him nude. He clasped the necklace in one hand, covering the pendant that read Ratha. He narrowed his eyes and stared at her. "What do you know of my necklace?" he asked warily.

"Only that it is the key to a door," she replied with a wink. "And that if you are searching for it, all you must do is tell me and I will divulge more."

"Very well," Argonal admitted. "I am searching for the archway that the elves of Ugram call the Infinat."

"Ha!" she crowed. "Infinat, indeed! A corruption of an old name, a name that came before men or elves ever walked Zaan. But that great iron arch is as ancient as the sun, old as the Orbidium itself. You can be certain old Oka knows where it lies."

"So?" asked Argonal. "Where does it lie?"

"That would be telling!" Oka said with a gap-toothed smile. "And I cannot do that without a prize or a price."

"A price!" Argonal said angrily. "I saved your life!"

"You did, but the archway is worth far more than any single life alone," she responded. "It is a thing of great magic, and so I will need a great magic in return."

Argonal glared at her and then unhooked the vambrace from his left arm. He threw the inscribed armlet down at her feet and said, "There! When you wear this bracelet you shall never know hunger or thirst. It is written with the name of three princely demons, who are bound to do your command. It has many other powers beyond that, but I shall only describe them to you once we reach the arch!"

Oka grinned and rubbed her hands. "We will leave tomorrow; it is not far, but without me, you shall never find it."

***

The crone had a tendency to ramble as they walked. Combined with the constant tittering of Habernath, the noise had the effect of lending the empty desert a host of voices. Argonal thus kept himself prepared, his senses acute, in case any dark thing should leap from the sands to accost them. He maintained a constant simmer of power in his belly, felt the bile lick his throat, and was primed at every turn to fire forth a Lance of Light or Coronondo's Retort. Oka seemed to speak of everything and nothing. It was as though she had been silent for decades in the desert and now, finding someone to speak to, a great dam had been burst and her ramblings spilled forth to slosh over sand and sky both.

Argonal paid her little attention. On the fourth day he had grown tired of eating her stewed rat and cave bat, filling though it was. He growled at Habernath and did his best to keep his anger from showing. He wondered if she meant to lead him to some inhospitable place, make him weak with slow starvation, and strip his body of all its treasures. She would find that even a stick-thin magician dying of thirst or hunger was more than enough to overmatch her. But at dusk that day he saw it: the sweep of the iron arch that Olomeryn had called the Infinat. On the far side, he knew, was the library of Ratha. He shivered that night in his sleep and dreamt of himself a thousand thousand miles high, knitting together the broken Orbidium with his bare hands. He closed the Cosmic Devoid with a single pinch and brought peace to Zaan.

When he woke, Oka was already prepared to go. She said, "No time for breaking fasts. The Infinat waits for us. And the serpent men."

"Serpent men?" Argonal ground his teeth. "Why did you not speak of them before?"

She shrugged. "This is the Desert of Horx. Surely you knew this was their dwelling place."

"In ages past, woman! They have all died out or retreated beyond the bounds of the known world, or else become moronic!" He fumed. He should have known. Not a day had gone by when he didn't think of the serpent men as they must have been when first they came to Zaan, the elder race that had raised the iron arches and great arks. "I had as much thought to meet a serpent man here as a dwarf!"

Oka pinched her grotesque face into a scrunch of thought. "They come when it pleases them and leave when they are finished. They may not be there. I thought it best that you be ready in case they dance beneath the arch tonight."

He knew he had no cause to be angry at Oka, but he was anyway. Habernath thought the whole exchange hilarious beyond words and constantly flitted between them, laughing. Argonal was accustomed to such antics by now, having lived with the scutling for nearly his entire adult life. Such hideous beasts were common in the Magician's City. All wizards in the realms of men studied magic at the knees of such monstrosities. Indeed, you could not call yourself truly a magician until you could reach into the space between spaces and yank forth a little demon of rank to tutor you in the obscene secrets of the art.

So instead of hurling his boot at Habernath (as he wanted to do) or shrieking at Oka (as his rage directed him) he simply staggered to his feet and began walking. Their approach took them through a brown gully that cut through the deep sandy rind of the desert's surface. Striations of color marked the walls, and drifts of red rust the floor. The arroyo did not twist or wind, but carried straight on. The sputtering red-white eye of the sun beat upon their backs with its feeble rays.

Argonal found himself tiring more easily each day. The powers of the vambrace had kept him moving, but now that it was gone he found Oka was the spry one and he was beset by aches and pains. The small of his back throbbed, his mouth was ever dry and dusty, and his eyesight sometimes blurred. He sipped occasionally from the waterskin Oka had given him. "You had best ensure I live to the arch," he muttered, "if you wish to know how to work that armband."

She twisted around to look at him. "Thirsty again? Your furnace burns bright, magician."

He nodded. "It is the magic within me," he explained. "I wear faster than other men if I keep it caged and waiting for use."

The goblin-faced woman laughed. "Against me, oh sage? You keep your spells in hand in case I turn on you?" She passed him another water skin.

The magician couldn't help but laugh. The power within him shifted like a stomach-full of serpents. "For whatever we may meet. Serpent men, you said."

She nodded and then fell silent. It was the first silence outside of nightfall she'd given him in days. He took that for a good omen. Habernath, of course, started muttering almost as soon as Oka stopped. He was whispering snatches of obscene poetry between warding spells and chants of seeing. Argonal was glad to see the scutling was taking no chances; perhaps he could afford to relax his vigil.

They could see the archway at the end of the canyon. It was framed by the rough stone walls and as they approached, Argonal got a true idea of its scale. It was titanic; twice the height of Ugram's mighty walls, and made of a rich gray iron. The sun glinted off of its surface and sheared into glimmering beams of light that played across the desert floor. From afar it seemed uniform, a great single and undivided mass of starborne iron stretching into the heavens. Yet as they approached it came into focus: whorls and shapes were graven upon its surface. Massive figures cavorted in strange serpentine splendor, twining and untwining within a frozen dance. He could feel the magic pouring off of it, even at this distance. It beat upon his brow like the heat of a second sun.

"It is much larger than I thought," Argonal called.

Oka laughed. "Have you never seen the Ark of Horx?"

He shook his head, dislodging sand that had fallen into his hair. He had never seen any of the great Arks. His study was limited to things from Zaan, not those that had slipped in from Outside. Well, he thought wryly, except for Habernath. He eyed the demon as it clutched its own paunch and muttered to itself.

"I have seen the Arks!" Habernath suddenly spouted. Argonal rolled his eyes. "I have, master!" The little demon's tone was the insistent whine of a child eager to be believed. "I have seen them all." He folded his arms and pouted his big wormlike lips.

Oka nodded at Habernath's outburst. "They scrape the very heavens."

Without warning the canyon fell away on either side. There was a straight way across the dunes to the Infinat and it seemed only a mile—or less. The archway was like a lodestone, drawing him ever closer. Argonal could not deny its pull, try though he might. The starborne iron was hammered with spells older than most of the races of Zaan. Only the dwarves had been sapient in the time before times when the Five Arks came screaming through the void and fell to Zaan. They were gone now, so there was no one left to question save the descendants of the serpent men themselves—and they had trouble remembering their own lifetimes, let alone those of their great ancestors.

Argonal turned to Oka. "You need go no further."

She nodded. "The band...?"

He sighed. Yes, of course this desert thief had not forgotten the rest of his promise. Not enough to be given the boon of eternal wellness, to require no food and no water. He rolled his eyes and began to explain the names of the three princes, the ways in which they could be called, and the other hidden powers of the ancient tool. "And never ever show it to an elf," he finished, "for it is of elven craft, and they will blast you to ash to recover it."

Oka said, "One last thing, magician," and her hideous bulging eyes bulged even wider. Argonal took a step back in surprise. "Would you go and defile one of our holy places with your human touch?" she asked, and her voice became a harsh rasp. Argonal stared in bafflement and Habernath began to shriek a cry of fright. "Would you paw at the relics made before you crawled from the sea, and wring some profit from them?" Oka's flesh began to slough from her arms and face, as though she were some animal in her stew. Where the gobbets of skin fell away, Argonal saw... scales. Brilliant, emerald scales. "You know this is our desert, man-thing. You know we own Horx."

Habernath took to the sky, spells of protection spilling from his mouth like a drunken man might vomit up his wine. Argonal found the fury in his gut pushing against his teeth, shining like a beacon from his throat. Coronondo's Retort exploded from his lips and he tasted the hot bile of magic. His eyes were lanterns, his hands were suns. Scintillating waves of light crashed over Oka. She flung them aside with one clawed hand.

"I am Okawere, and this is our land! All Zaan is ours, even if it is dying!" She reached out and ripped into his tunic. Her claws would easily have disemboweled him had Habernath's defensive magic not already woven a girdle about his waist. Instead, she shredded the cloth near his midsection with a powerful blow.

A Lance of Light appeared on his tongue; he shaped the words to give it life, felt the fire in him blazing hot. The furnace of his belly was stoked. The lance ripped from between his lips and shot through Okawere's side, ripping a hole the size of a fist from her sinuous form. She fell back even as Habernath landed on her face, his own lips a blazing sheet of fire. When at last the little demon rose, he pouted again. "That was too near!" he complained.

Argonal cleared his head, drank from his waterskin, and then laughed and retrieved the vambrace from Okawere's smoking form. "Now I, like you, need no food and no drink again."

Habernath groaned his displeasure as they began walking again. The archway seemed to shimmer in the afternoon light. Argonal thought he saw strange scribblings of light passing between the towering arms of the gate. The amulet around his neck began to feel warm to the touch, as though a second living heart was beating in time with his. As they drew nearer he knew he could not be mistaken: purple scrollwork was now shooting between the great bands of deep gray iron. He smiled and strode forward with purpose, Habernath trailing behind like an errant thought.

***

"Dinner was... pleasant," Olomeryn admitted. The splashing of the fountain echoed through the high-ceilinged chamber. Nibenlibe inclined his head, giving the appearance of a seated bow.

"Thank you, my dear," he said. "I marvel that you had such free time. Surely you would normally have spent an evening such as this, all the moons in full, with your human lover?"

Olomeryn despised Nibenlibe and it was only the slow catatonia of her race that prevented her from taking more deliberate action. But the social dance was integral to living in great Ugram, so she was silent for a moment. She needed to collect herself before admitting the truth to foul Nibenlibe. "He has not returned," she said. To her credit her voice did not waver at all.

"Ah," said Nibenlibe, feigning sadness. "That is a shame." He looked even more putridly handsome in the light of the black candles burning on the table, she thought, than he normally did beneath the amber glow of the crystal lamps. Behind him the thin curtains rustled, barely concealing the brilliant display of the equinox. "Perhaps he grew tired of you. Humans can be unpredictable, changeable things."

She could feel tears, real tears, behind her eyes. She had not cried since she was a child, innumerable centuries ago. "I doubt that is the reason," she said, and she kept the emotion from her voice. She was sure Nibenlibe could see the strain in her eyelids and would already think himself courting victory. "He is most likely dead." There! Her voice had remained steady as iron.

"Oh?" asked Nibenlibe. Amusement played across his face. She had the sudden inkling that he was concealing something. She had known him, hated him, for far too long not to recognize that. "What would make you think that? Had he gone somewhere... dangerous?"

She narrowed her eyes instinctively, unable to control it. She cursed herself for revealing her suspicions so openly. An unforgivable lapse! "He went to find the Library of Ratha," she said. There was no use dissembling when he asked her a question so baldly. Just as she could read the lines of a lie in his face, he could read hers.

He stood up, pushing back his onyx chair. He turned away from her, and she detected a hint of a smile in his voice. "Oh? Is that where my necklace had gone? You stole it from me that night? I have been wondering these past years."

"Yes," she said, and suddenly the tears could no longer be held at bay. A few forerunners trickled down her face, which she quickly wiped away on her sleeve. His back was turned, she thought, he did not see. "The night you told me of the Infinat."

"Ah," he said, and his voice was rich with knowing. "Yes, of course. He went through the Infinat with my necklace." He turned back around and she saw that his face was transported with rapture. He reached down to scoop his silver goblet from the table. There was a silence as they faced each other and then he took a sip of wine and asked, "Did it never occur to you why it was so easy to get the necklace? Or to get the location of the Infinat from me?" he asked.

"Never," she said hoarsely. She could feel her body betraying her, and for an instant she didn't even want it to obey. She dabbed at her eyes, and she didn't care that Nibenlibe saw her doing it. "I never questioned it."

"Nor were you meant to," Nibenlibe agreed. "And I told you so many truths. Indeed, I think perhaps your lover is still there on Flux to this day, in that library."

"What do you mean?" she asked, and milky tears streamed now without abandon down her cheeks.

"Surely you stopped to think," he said with a wry grin, "That so close to the Devoid no space-bending magics could function?" He shook his head. "Ah dear, Olomeryn. You did not even stop to consider it? I suppose your lover did not either. To be sure, there is said to be another gate on Flux like the one in the desert, but I fear that using it would spell certain doom! The lines of force would become all twisted, and anyone who passed from the tunnel that way would almost assuredly be flensed and pulped like a rat in a meat grinder."

Olomeryn wept. Long ragged breaths escaped from her throat and she began to make a low moaning noise. For a moment, just a moment, she thought of unleashing her sorcerous fury on him. She could call upon every pact ever made by her ancestors, summon up the allegiance of every fiend of hell, pour forth a torrent of spellfire and hatred onto him and obliterate him utterly. But it was only for a moment, for Olomeryn knew that Nibenlibe also had a storehouse of magical knowledge surrounding him. Were she to bring it to physical combat, who could say if she would win? And though the thought of personal annihilation no longer frightened her, she could not bear the thought that she would die and he would not. So she did nothing but weep and moan.

"Ah, my dear Olomeryn," Nibenlibe said sadly. "I remember how this all began, so long ago. Now, perhaps, you shall finally admit that the vintage made from my grapes—the vintage of which you have partaken every time you have been a guest in my house!—is actually quite good, and not foul at all."

Olomeryn dutifully raised her goblet to her mouth and took a sip of Nibenlibe's wine—the cursed wine, which she had once been so haughty as to declare slightly acidic—and nodded. "It is not bitter at all," she said in a small voice. "It is not bitter at all."

THE GOD IN THE URN
MATTHEW BOTTIGLIERI

"And how are Hrulvir's finest sellswords faring this evening?" said Dmitri the moneylender.

"We are well," said a massive Red Islander named Jarvos.

"You must loathe this peace, though." Dmitri swatted a fly with an ivory whip.

"As much as you love it, probably," said a short, aquiline warrior with pale hair and mismatched eyes. His name was Gaunt.

Dmitri smiled. "It makes no difference to me. I prosper whether men kill one another or not." He clapped his hands and a eunuch at least seven feet tall lifted him like a sack of flour and draped him over a dark shoulder.

Jarvos was amazed at how strong the eunuch was, for Dmitri was morbidly obese. He looked like a slug wrapped in gold silk.

Dmitri said, "We shall dine together in my arboretum whilst we talk of more pressing matters."

The arboretum was a veritable forest enclosed in glass. Birds flew above their heads as Jarvos watched the eunuch place Dmitri upon a cushion that reminded him of scrambled eggs. A group of boys bearing trays heaping with eel that had been marinated in olive oil and seared in garlic entered the arboretum and set the food on covered tables. Jarvos and Gaunt ate their fill of eel, leeks, and mushrooms, and washed the meal down with wine. Jarvos had not eaten so well in as long as he could remember. After listening to Dmitri prattle about which trees were susceptible to which malady, as well as the species of birds that he'd captured, the merchant clapped his hands and the boys removed the trays. "And now, let's get to the heart of the matter." Dmitri stroked the head of a lime-colored bird that landed upon his wrist. "Have the two of you ever heard of the Cult of Jun-Nabbath?"

"Everyone's heard of those maggot worshippers." Gaunt scratched his nape. "What of them?"

Dmitri laughed and clapped his hands. "Well-put, Gaunt! It just so happens that these maggot-worshippers possess an artifact that I'm interested in acquiring." His tiny eyes gleamed like wet onyx.

Jarvos crossed his arms. "Have you tried buying it from them?"

Dmitri's smile melted. "There are certain things that one cannot buy, no matter how much money one offers." A very peculiar look flashed across his face for a moment. "Be that as it may, if you know anything about me, you know that I always get what I want – one way or another."

"What is this artifact, exactly?" Jarvos watched the bird fly from Dmitri's shoulder and land on the branch of a nearby tree.

"An urn," said Dmitri. "It resembles brass, but I assure you that it is not composed of any substance known to man. It is older than iron. It is older than the mountains – the seas, even. It may be older than the world itself." He dragged a sharp finger through his beard. "While the market is soft for such curios, the urn is extremely valuable for other... esoteric reasons." The usurer chuckled.

Jarvos felt like Dmitri had just insulted him, but he couldn't figure out how. "This job is more complicated than setting fire to a rival's warehouse or breaking bones."

"It will cost more, in other words?" Dmitri laughed. "Don't be such a piker, Jarvos. Speak frankly."

Gaunt said, "I've heard all sorts of rumors about this cult. I've heard that they feast upon the dead and perform awful rituals upon any who are caught trespassing within their sanctum."

"Yes, yes, I know the rumors as well," said Dmitri. "I'm not as credulous as you two, however. These folk simply worship a forgotten deity. Their rituals are bizarre because they are so old. I am sure that they're as harmless as any of the other myriad religions in Hrulvir." Dmitri threaded his fingers together. "Be that as it may, I am prepared to make the two of you quite wealthy if you carry out this task." As if on cue, eunuchs appeared bearing mahogany chests reinforced with iron. They opened the lids and golden eels and precious gems spilled onto the grass.

Jarvos licked his lips and stared at the flood of riches. The smile upon Dmitri's face felt mocking and condescending, but he didn't care. He smiled at Gaunt, who seemed to have the same stupefied expression upon his scarred face.

"I have no idea how much gold is in those chests," said Dmitri. "I do know, however, that they contain more gold and jewels than you're likely to see again." He paused a moment and then said, "You could easily pay off the gambling debt that you owe to that thug Balthazar, and have plenty left over to do whatever you like. You could spend a year drinking lotus nectar all day; even better, you could gamble the money away and become indebted to Balthazar all over again."

"How do you know about our debt?" said Jarvos.

Dmitri rolled his eyes. "You're far too large and imposing to play coy, Jarvos." Dmitri coughed into his fist. "If you think I earned this wealth without knowing everything about everyone, you're more foolish than I thought." Dmitri's tongue slid across his teeth. "So, do we have a deal?"

***

The Cult of Jun-Nabbath resided in a crumbling tower in the Narrows, a seedy neighborhood in southwest Hrulvir. Like the Foreign Quarter, thin streets flanked by abandoned flats and tenement slums cut across one another and ended abruptly in dead ends. Alleyways marred the streets like fissures in a pockmarked face. The Narrows was one of the oldest regions of Hrulvir, since it spread like an infection from the River Hrul, and was once the home of men and women who fished for massive river eels.

"Aren't you from the Narrows?" Jarvos wore a cloak over a leather tunic, eel skin breeches, and high boots. A massive broadsword and a coil of rope were slung across his back.

"You've asked me this question many times before," said Gaunt. "The answer is yes. I was in fact born in this cesspit, but I found my way out as early as possible." The short man had looped his hair into knot behind his head. His eel skin leggings and tunic were dyed the color of blood, and were riveted with silver studs. A short cloak of dark wool billowed from his shoulders, and a pair of curved blades dangled from his belt.

"That explains why it took you so long to figure out where we're going." Jarvos drank deeply from a wineskin and handed it to Gaunt.

They crouched in an alley and watched pale moonlight spill across the tower's ancient brick. It leaned with age, but it was still sturdy. Most of the windows that zigzagged up its hundred-foot length were either broken or boarded up. The base of the tower was cordoned off by a wall ten feet high and five feet thick. The wall was in better shape than the tower, and was probably of more recent construction. Jarvos neither saw nor heard anyone; the silence was eerie. The tower languished adjacent to an abandoned church of Groan, which had been built back when the Narrows was a decent place to live.

"I'm surprised that the Church of Groan would allow this cult to exist alongside it..."

"The church was probably abandoned long before the cult invaded that tower," said Gaunt.

"I have an idea," said Jarvos.

***

The door to the abandoned temple yielded when Jarvos rammed it with his shoulder. The sell-swords entered a long rectangular chapel that was covered in a thick film of dust. The temple had long since been looted. The statue of Groan had been toppled and the head had been removed. Pigeons cooed and fluttered in the rafters above their heads. There were a myriad number of gods worshipped throughout Hrulvir, but Groan was probably the most prominent of the eclectic pantheon – especially among the older citizens of the city. In addition to Groan, many worshipped Mitra of the Blue Shroud, the Silent Mother, Shivas the Destroyer. No one that Jarvos knew worshipped Jun-Nabbath.

Jarvos and Gaunt climbed a staircase that spiraled to the top of the temple. The stairs buckled and splintered beneath their weight on more than one occasion. They ascended to the belfry and scuttled onto a sagging roof, pausing for a few moments to admire the view. Hrulvir's decrepit cityscape spread in every direction. The winking lights below glittered like the coins and jewels that had spilled from Dmitri's chest; though there was probably greater wealth in that chest than in all The Narrows. The River Hrul slithered through the center of the city like a great eel. The eleven hills of Hrulvir's Hilltop district were illuminated by flickering lights framed in thousands of windows. To Jarvos, the spires of the Overlord's palace threatened to slip from the peak of the tallest hill like a crown from an old man's head. The stink of Isle Town wafted them from the south, where the Hrul emptied into the Bleak Sea and the harbor bristled with masts. It was an archipelago of taverns, gambling dens, brothels, and rotting warehouses that sprouted like cancer from a stagnant lagoon.

"Such an ugly city," said Gaunt, spitting.

Jarvos smiled. "You should see the Red Isles, if you want to see true ugliness."

Gaunt smiled, "If your people look anything like you, I can imagine."

Jarvos smiled through the tattoos of his face. "You'd love the women, Gaunt. They're as tall as I am."

They moved gingerly across what was left of the roof and peered down at the top of the tower twenty feet below them. Jarvos discerned a trap door in the roof. They tied rope to a weathered merlon, tested its strength, and let the rope drop to the roof of the tower. Jarvos uttered a prayer to his ancestral spirits and descended the rope. The muscles of his arms and legs swelled as he lowered himself. Gaunt had been gracious enough to allow him to go first, but Jarvos had demanded that they flip a coin for the honor. Jarvos lost.

"Move faster, you big baby," said Gaunt, descending above him. "You're too tall to be afraid of heights."

"Fool! You'll bring the church down upon us. Wait until I reach the bottom!" Jarvos landed upon the tiled roof and crouched. When he was certain that they had not been detected, he crept like a panther across the roof and pried open the trapdoor. He peered down a flight of stairs into utter darkness.

"I don't suppose you thought of bringing torches, did you?" Jarvos scratched the back of his neck.

"No," said Gaunt, drawing his curved blades. "Let's hope these maggots are as blind as we are in the dark."

Their eyes adjusted as they crept downward and entered a chamber that appeared to have been a library at some point in the past. The room was illuminated by three torches. The bookcases were empty, save for a few tomes with rotting spines. Gaunt opened one of them and the pages crumpled.

"I had no idea that you could read." The Red Islander crushed a spider with the heel of his boot.

"I can't," said Gaunt, "But one sometimes discovers maps and other secrets stashed within old books."

They followed another flight of stairs that spiraled downward into living quarters. The narrow window in the room was boarded with wood, and dirty sleeping mats were strewn across the floor. There were forty of them, at least. The reek of unwashed chamber pots threatened to overwhelm them. Gaunt kicked one of them as they searched the room. They found nothing of value. No urn, obviously.

They descended more stairs and crossed through more smelly dormitories. When they'd descended halfway down the tower, they entered a chamber completely covered in frescoes. It appeared to be a place of worship. The Frescoes depicted thousands of people groveling as a worm-like creature spiraled upwards and strangled a moon that was painted across the ceiling.

"That must be Jun-Nabbath," Gaunt poked the image with tip of one his blades. "What an awful-looking thing it is."

"I remember old women speaking about a mysterious tribe that lived on a small island beyond the reefs of the Red Islands. They supposedly worshipped a god that was thousands of years old," said Jarvos. "They observed strange rights and sacrificed sailors captured during pirate raids. Jarvos peered at Jun-Nabbath. "Perhaps this god is akin to the god that those island savages worshipped. Their image certainly differs. The god of the islanders was a mass of tentacles and claws. I saw one of their totems once, when I was a child. Despite the differences, something about Jun-Nabbath reminds me of that elder thing of the island." Gooseflesh spread across his arms.

Doors suddenly opened like wounds in the walls and a dozen figures shrouded in phlegm-colored robes bled from the passages and surrounded Jarvos and Gaunt. One of the figures wore a robe with dark symbols etched across the sleeves and hood. "Who dares invade the sanctum of Jun-Nabbath?" he said.

Jarvos said nothing.

The speaker drew a curved dagger of dark metal and said, "Maggots shall feast upon you. Get them!"

Jarvos beheaded the first acolyte who laid hands upon him. The body spewed blood from its neck and collapsed. The Red Islander kicked the severed head across the room and then slipped in the blood as curved blades slashed him from every direction. He saw Gaunt whirl his blades, spilling innards, and darting like a ferret between filthy-robed attackers. Jarvos dropped his blade in pain as a twisted knife licked his neck. He smashed the face of a cultist who bit his shoulder. Then two more bore Jarvos down and crawled on top of him. He tore their hoods from their heads as he struggled to free himself and gagged when he stared into eyeless faces and black teeth bristling behind lipless mouths. He kicked, punched, and growled as he threw the acolytes from him and struggled to his feet. He head-butted one and felt bones crush like rotting fruit. He snatched his sword as he rolled to his feet. Then he twisted desperately to his right to avoid a thrust and the knife merely grazed his chest instead of impaling his heart. They slew the rest, but the leader slipped through one of the doors before they could stop him. They bled from a dozen slashes, but none of them were deep.

Gaunt wiped his blades and said, "I'm getting old."

Jarvos leaned upon his blade. "That makes two of us." He said, panting. "I need to quit drinking and whoring so much."

"Where's the fun in that?" The little man smiled as he caught his breath. "They're alive and we're dead; we're as young as we need to be." He urinated on one of the corpses.

They descended stairways that snaked and twisted around one another. Some terminated in dead ends and abandoned rooms. They found chambers filled with bones. They found flayed torsos dangling from rusted hooks, and another room that was filled with shriveled hands. They saw the hight priest slip behind a tapestry hanging from a wall on the ground floor. They ran after him, but the priest was gone by the time they peered behind the tapestry and found a flight of stairs that lead below ground.

The walls enclosing the stairwell were defaced by the same images that were in the ritual chamber above. The catacombs at the bottom of the stairs branched to the east and west. They crept along the eastern passage, down a hall lined with pillars carved to resemble the writhing shape of Jun-Nabbath. Torches flickering in wall sconces cast weird vermiform shadows. Jarvos caught a glimpse of movement to his left and spun to face it just as a cultist flung himself at him from behind a column, screaming and slashing at him with a dagger and gouging his bicep. Jarvos pinned the cultist to one of the columns and slit his throat. As this happened, a panel in the floor opened and a robed figure rose from the floor and almost disemboweled Gaunt; the flaxen-haired bravo dodged the parried the attacker's slash and rammed his blade through the cultist's eye.

They entered a hallway with a dozen barred cells on either side. They peered through bars and beheld cells that reeked of excrement and were crammed with skeletal prisoners. Jarvos said, "They were probably drunks and vagrants who were dragged kicking and screaming from the streets above us, to be tortured and eaten." All of the prisoners were missing limbs, as well as other extremities. Some attempted to see with empty sockets. Jarvos gagged when he spied maggots squirm from festering lacerations. The smell made him vomit. His wished to release those poor wretches from their misery, but the doors were locked.

At the end of the hallway, they came upon a double-paneled door of gold with images of torture engraved upon it. Men and women much like those that Jarvos had seen languishing in cells were disemboweled by robed figures wielding implements that seemed designed specifically for that purpose. They passed through the doors and entered an octagonal room that was twenty feet in diameter. Flames danced in tarnished sconces and cast shadows across mosaics depicting the same tableau that they'd witnessed before: human-like figures groveling beneath a maggot that coiled about the moon and fed upon it.

Prayer mats were strewn across the tiled floor, and a stone slab roughly six feet long had been constructed in the center of the room. Its surface, as well as the floor beneath it, was stained. A row of barbed knives and hooks dangled from the walls. The urn was perched upon a dais made of bones that were threaded together with dried blood and sinew. Hair streamed from a skull wearing a crown made of ribs.

Jarvos studied the profane images that were engraved upon the vessel and sensed that the relic that was older than he could fathom. He couldn't tell if the metal looked like gold, or bronze, or something else entirely. His hands shook when he placed the urn in an old sack and slung it over his shoulder.

"Let's get out of here now," said Gaunt.

They became lost within dim passages that Jarvos swore had

changed since he and Gaunt had found the urn, but he pressed forward. Then this nape bristled as they crept down a long hallway carved with bas-reliefs depicting shrouded figures feeding upon the dead. Jarvos heard stone slide against stone and several alcoves opened along the hallway. Jarvos impaled the priest that sprung from the opening on his right and sliced his face with a curved dagger. He wiped blood from his eyes and attempted to aid Gaunt, who struggled with two cultists, but the cultist that he'd just impaled grabbed a hold of his legs and tripped him. Jarvos gasped for air, for the fall had knocked the wind out of him. He shattered the cultist's jaw with the heel of his boot, after he'd caught his breath. A slashing knife removed the tip of Jarvos's ear. He smashed the cultist's head against the wall until the skull was crushed.

The two cultists attacking Gaunt slashed his cloak and stabbed his arms and midsection. The little man's scimitar counterattack disemboweled one of the cultists. The other's dagger bit into Gaunt's back before the little man beheaded him.

"Run, now!" Jarvos grabbed Gaunt by what was left of his cloak and dragged him down the passageway.

Several more cultists lunged from hidden alcoves, but Jarvos and Gaunt sprinted past them and sprinted down a perpendicular passage way. Jarvos was intent upon fleeing those accursed catacombs. Even Hrulvir's foul air was better than the reek of that subterranean maze. They ran for a long while until they outdistanced their attackers. At one point, they passed what appeared to Jarvos to be a kennel of some sort. Through bars, they saw goads and whips dangling from hooks. A swarm of flies hovered over a heap of offal rotting in a trough.

"What sort of beast could these maggots breed in this shit hole?" Gaunt leaned against the wall and caught his breath.

"Something loathsome," said Jarvos.

The high priest swung his club as they rounded the next corner. The blow missed Jarvos's head by inches. Jarvos attempted to swing his sword, but the priest kneed his groin and clutched his throat. Jarvos dropped his blade and grabbed the hand wrapped around his throat and attempted to break fingers. He never had the opportunity, for Gaunt's blade clove the priest's hand at the wrist. The priest screamed and clutched his stump with his other hand. Jarvos raised his blade to kill the priest.

"Let him bleed to death!" Gaunt stood at the end of the hallway. "Let's get out of here."

Jarvos took one last look at the high priest before they rounded another bend and noticed that he'd put a whistle to his mouth. The whistle's high pitch carved through their ears as they ran down the hallway. Jarvos wondered if the priest had attempted to summon more cultists. Then a screech unlike any other he'd ever heard before echoed off the walls and sent a shudder scuttling up his spine. The wail reminded Jarvos of the chirping of locusts, but there was something slimy about it as well. It stopped him in mid stride the next time they heard it. They continued to sprint through unfamiliar passages, having forsaken caution so that they could escape as quickly as possible.

"Something follows us," said Gaunt, peering behind him. "I can hear claws scraping across stone."

"You're hearing things," said Jarvos, groping along the wall.

Then chittering scream was much louder when they reached the stairs. Something heavy and wet landed on Jarvos's back when he tripped on the stairs and smashed his knee on a stone step. He screamed as he felt teeth and claws tear his neck and his back. "Get it off me!" He attempted to rise but creature's bulk pinned him to the stairs.

He heard Gaunt scream a battle cry, then the thing on his back roared in agony and tumbled over itself down the stairs. He caught a glimpse of scuttling legs, a white bulk, and the gnashing of slimy incisors. Gaunt yanked him to his feet and they hacked their way through a boarded up door on the ground floor and sprinted across a crumbling courtyard. They found the strength to scale the wall faster than they could believe and they vanished into the alleys and crumbling tenements.

***

Although Dmitri's explicit orders were to return the urn as soon as they retrieved it, Jarvos and Gaunt stopped at Madam Nu's lotus parlor on the Avenue of Moths. The old madam glared at them as they limped through her front door and slid behind the curtains of one of the booths. They set the urn upon the table between them.

"You're going to bleed all over my cushions," said Nu, an ancient dowager who claimed to be royalty from the Empire of Mist.

Jarvos wiped blood from his forehead, "Lotus, please."

Nu stared at the urn. "How will you pay for it?"

"We'll settle up with you later this evening. If I told you what we've been through earlier tonight, you'd drink lotus nectar along with us."

Nu brought them nectar mixed with wine. It was weak, but they drank it without complaint. Their wounds stopped throbbing, but their sense of disgust lingered.

They spent what felt like hours in a torpor and failed to notice the silver-haired man attired completely in black leather that entered the parlor. His nose looked like it'd been flattened with a hammer. He was short and compact like an Illanese fighting dog, and he wore short blades at his hips. If Jarvos had been thinking straight, he would've requested a private room, but it was too late for such considerations. The man smiled when he spotted Jarvos and nodded to the three warriors from that stood behind him. Jarvos knew them well. They were triplets with a legendary proclivity for violence. They were known as the Scorpion Brothers, for they each bore a tattoo of a scorpion upon their left forearm. Muscle swelled beneath their leather vests and dark breeches. Large swords hung from their hips.

The man with flat face parted the curtain and said, "May I?"

"Hello, Balthazar." Jarvos, scratched his head.

Balthazar squatted upon a cushion opposite them and rested his elbows on the table. "You look like hell – both of you." His eyes gleamed like jade. "Hopefully you've bled all over yourselves scrounging up the gold you owe me." The edge of his mouth twitched when he spotted the sack that was next to Jarvos. Balthazar motioned and one of his stooges reached into the bag and removed the urn and handed it to Balthazar.

"What the hell is this thing?" Balthazar flipped it with his scarred hands.

"None of your business," said Gaunt.

Balthazar laughed. "Did you hear that?" The triplets smiled and revealed sharpened teeth. "This thing looks old, but something tells it's worth a lot of money." He started to pry the lid from the top of it. Jarvos knocked his hand away.

Balthazar's face froze. "You ever touch me again and I'll tear your fucking head off." The three brothers brushed the hilts of their swords. Balthazar put the urn on the table and folded his arms across his chest, "Where's the gold that you owe me?"

"We'll have it for you in a few hours," said Jarvos.

"I was supposed to have it last week," Balthazar ground his teeth and stood up. "If you don't bring me my gold by midnight, I'll feed you to my eels." He tucked the urn underneath his arm.

Jarvos attempted to stop him, but the three brothers formed a wall of sharpened teeth and bristling muscle.

"Now I know it's worth something," Balthazar smiled and tapped the lid of the container. "This should take care of today's interest." He tossed the urn to one of the brothers. "Perhaps you can tell me where you found it when you deliver my gold this evening." One of the Scorpions spit in Jarvos's wine.

***

"And I thought I'd hired capable men," Dmitri tore ivory pins from his hair and let it spill down his shoulders. Although streaked with grey, much of it was still as dark as a horse's tail.

Jarvos had never seen the merchant this angry before. "You don't understand," he said. "Balthazar was accompanied by all three Scorpion Brothers. They bathe in children's blood before going into battle. We're brave, but we're not stupid."

"Spare me," Dmitri bore his teeth and held up a creased palm. The boy who fanned him got a little bit too close and Dmitri pushed him into a fountain. Jarvos watched him feverishly comb his hair with an ivory brush; his saffron robe slipped from his shoulders.

Jarvos averted his eyes. "We are deeply sorry that we've disappointed you."

Dmitri sighed. "By the looks of it, the two of you had quite an interesting night. You're both covered in blood and who knows what else."

"You don't know the half of it." Gaunt attempted to conceal a smile.

"It angers me that you didn't follow my simple instructions." Dmitri snapped the neck of the bird that was perched on his wrist and threw the carcass at Jarvos. "If you'd returned the urn to me forthwith, rather than stop off at that revolting parlor, you'd have enough wealth to open seven parlors of your own!" The merchant struggled to his feet; his robe tore from his body and exposed his pale, obese nudity. He lifted the chair that he'd been sitting on and threw it. Six eunuchs entered the arboretum after he clapped three times. Each of them wore nothing but a linen loincloth and sandals. They were desert warriors from the Dead God's Palm. "If you think Balthazar's dangerous, feast your eyes on them." Dmitri unsheathed a terrifying smile as he approached Jarvos, grabbed his face with both hands, and kissed him on the lips. "I don't care how you do it, but you and that piece of trash that you call your friend will get that urn back from Balthazar." He patted Jarvos on the cheek and clapped his hands. One of the eunuchs scooped him up in his massive arms. "I'd loan you my men, but I have enemies of my own, you see, and they are far more powerful than Balthazar." The merchant laughed as the eunuch held him like baby. "We're in this together, boys." The eunuch carried him from the arboretum. "If you fail, feel free to kill yourselves."

***

"I've thought of fleeing, too, but there's no place to run." Jarvos finished his mug of wine and wiped his mouth with the back of his hand. "Dmitri will hire assassins to hunt us down no matter where we hide."

"I know," said Gaunt. "And Balthazar will remove our bollocks if he catches us."

"What choice do we have?" Jarvos smashed his mug against the table.

Gaunt shrugged.

They left the Gilded Tortoise, a rundown tavern in an eastside slum called the Tannery, and made their way towards Balthazar's squat. His flat-roofed villa was surrounded by an unsightly grey wall and a rusted iron gate. Like Balthazar, it was short, menacing, and served no purpose. The wall was cracked and strangled with weeds, which made it easy for Jarvos and Gaunt to climb a section that was bathed in darkness. They perched on top of it like a pair of crows. Moonlight spilled across a courtyard of bleached tile and weeds.

"It looks like we won't have to worry about Balthazar's dogs after all," said Gaunt.

They dropped into the courtyard and they remained still for several seconds. Balthazar's three fighting dogs – squat, hairless brutes with shark mouths - lay dead across the cracked tiles. There were robed figures there as well – six of them.

Something else lay dead as well - a pale, segmented monstrosity with hundreds of legs and a dark mouth full of needle-like teeth. The dogs had managed to kill it as it killed them.

"I never liked those dogs," said Jarvos.

"They didn't like you either," Gaunt drew his blades.

"They didn't even like Balthazar, I don't think," said Jarvos, drawing his blade.

"Nobody likes Balthazar." Gaunt stared at the dead cultists. "How in the ninety-nine hells would the cult have known to come here?"

"This thing followed the urn, I think" said Jarvos, nudging the disgusting creature with his boot. "I don't know how or why, but it followed the urn like a dog follows a scent. Perhaps this is the thing that attacked me on the stairs." He choked back the bile that crept into his throat.

The front door of Balthazar's villa had been wrenched from its hinges, and Jarvos found one of the Scorpion Brothers slumped in the middle of a long hallway. Several cultists lay in a heap around him, dead. The brother held his guts in place with bloodstained hands. When he saw Jarvos and Gaunt, he cursed and spat blood from his ruined mouth; Gaunt rammed his blade through his throat.

They stepped over robed bodies as they skulked down the hallway and entered a gaudy throne room. At least two dozen robed priests were strewn across the tiled floor along with the rest of Balthazar's men. His harem of painted whores had been hacked to pieces along with several of his lackeys. Jarvos recognized a few Red Island cutthroats, as well as an assassin from the Empire of Mist, a horse thief from the Golden Steppes, and an Illaran pimp with gold teeth. Another Scorpion Brother lay dead with brains bulging from a smashed skull. At the opposite side of the room, gigantic black eels thrashed and fought over the body of the high priest which floated in the filthy water.

Jarvos found the urn next to Balthazar's throne. He had the urn in hand when Balthazar limped into the room, accompanied by the last of the brothers. The man's lip quivered when he saw Jarvos and Gaunt. He drew his blades and said, "Kill them both."

The brother, seven feet of scarred muscle, raised a double-bladed axe and advanced. Jarvos was nearly as tall as his opponent, but he was leaner. The scorpion smiled and swung his axe as soon as Jarvos was within range. The Red Islander parried the blow and felt his shoulder snap from its socket. He gritted his teeth and switched hands. He barely dodged the brother's next chop, and he swung his sword as hard as he could, but he was swinging with his off-hand, and the blow was clumsy. The scorpion parried the attack and grinned. Jarvos swung again and the scorpion wrenched the sword from his hand and smashed Jarvos's nose with his elbow.

Jarvos sank to his knees and clutched his nose. "Come on, you Red Island cunt. Is that all you got? I've raped whores with more fight in them than you," said the Scorpion.

Jarvos moaned when he took a boot to his ribs; he bit his lip when the scorpion tore the rings from his ears.

"You like pretty earrings, you little bitch?" The axe clattered to the floor. "I only use my axe on men, not on little bitches."

Jarvos lunged, then. He had no idea where he found the strength to spring to his feet, but he shot under the Scorpion's guard and rammed his left shoulder into his gut. The warrior groaned and stumbled backwards and tripped over a corpse and fell in the pool. He tried to climb out, but the eels coiled around him and dragged him into the filthy water.

Balthazar smiled through smashed lips as Jarvos advanced upon him from the left and Gaunt flanked Balthazar on the right. Balthazar lunged at Jarvos and slithered in close so that the Red Islander couldn't hit him with his sword; he buried his dagger in Jarvos's hip and smashed his chin with his forehead.

Warm blood seeped from Jarvos's side when he came to. His jaw felt shattered. He clutched his wound and watched Gaunt and Balthazar circle one another. It was clear that Gaunt had taken worse than he'd given, but Balthazar bled from his midsection, and had cuts along his arms and legs. Jarvos hated Balthazar, but he respected him as well.

Gaunt swung at Balthazar's head, but the thug drove his shoulder into Gaunt's midsection and knocked him back several feet. Jarvos looked for his sword but it was on the opposite side of the room. He saw the urn, however, and he picked it up and crept towards Balthazar as he slithered past Gaunt's guard and pinned his arms to his side. He cursed Balthazar when he shoved Gaunt against the wall and tore a hunk of flesh from his cheek and spat it in his face. The Red Islander ground his teeth and the urn smashed down on Balthazar's head.

***

Dmitri received them in his front parlor. He wore a lime-colored robe and he roosted upon a lounge with wooden arms curved to resemble waves. Beautiful watercolor paintings purchased from the Empire of Mist adorned the room's eight walls. A gilded tapestry of the heavens hung like a canopy from the ceiling. Dmitri clapped when he saw the urn.

"Forget everything I said about you." He held the the urn with his manicured fingers. "You are both my favorite mercenaries again." He looked at Jarvos quizzically when he noticed the dried blood that was caked to the bottom of the urn. "I trust that Balthazar is dead, then?"

Jarvos nodded.

"Splendid!" Dmitri smiled. "Hrulvir will be all the better for it." Dmitri handed the urn to a eunuch, but the vessel slipped between his hands and cracked the tiled floor. "Dog!" Dmitri punched the top of the servant's head as he bent down and retrieved the urn and placed it next to a vase that exploded with orchids. Jarvos watched the eunuch retreat until his back touched the wall; hatred gleamed in his eyes.

A serving boy in a tourmaline-colored robe entered and poured Jarvos and Gaunt wine. When their cups were full, Dmitri raised his glass and said, "A toast to the finest sell-swords in Hrulvir. May you live out the remainder of your insignificant lives in peace and comfort." The merchant set his wine next to the urn. Jarvos hadn't eaten or drank anything in hours, so he emptied his wine glass and smiled when the boy refilled it. Gaunt followed suit. The wine was delicious - a tad bitter, but delicious nonetheless.

"You must be eager to collect your reward." Dmitri clapped three times and eight eunuchs entered the room. Two more entered bearing chests and stood beside Dmitri. Dmitri's face, powdered, was as pale as death. His smile cracked the white plaster that was annealed to his face, but there was no mirth in his eyes.

The glass slid from Jarvos's hand and shattered upon the tiled floor as the eunuchs opened the lids. The chests were empty. He tried to speak but his lips were asleep and his tongue felt as heavy as lead. He heard Gaunt crash to the floor, but he could barely move his eyes. The last thing he remembered was the darkness of Dmitri's eyes. They gleamed as lustrously as black pearls and threatened to devour him. Jarvos had glimpsed that expression before, but now he felt as though the merchant had finally revealed a facet of his personality that he concealed from him for all the years that he'd performed errands for him. Jarvos wanted to tear his eyes from that hideous expression, but he couldn't, no matter how hard he tried.

***

"You must be aware of the fact that there are nobler pursuits than the acquisition of wealth." Dmitri pulled a scroll from a hollow femur and unfurled it.

"I don't care to listen to your prattling. If you're going to kill us, get on with it!" Jarvos strained against the ropes which coiled around him. Gaunt was similarly trussed.

"I've never seen you put a wine cup down without emptying it first," said Jarvos. "I should've known that something was amiss when you didn't drink the wine that was poured in your glass."

Dmitri smiled. "You were too busy thinking about chests full of gold." The merchant preened his fingernails with a golden knife. "I am doing you a favor, you know. If I let you live, you'll spend the rest of your life indebted to one crime boss or another."

Jarvos peered across Dmitri's shoulder and saw they were in a high chamber and guessed that they were at the top of the slender tower that was adjacent to Dmitri's manse. He'd never been in the tower before, but be knew what it was used for. He guessed that they'd been carried here by Dmitri's eunuchs after the poison had done its work. He had no idea how long they'd slumbered at the top of the tower. It might have been days, for all he knew.

The bookshelves which lined the walls were crammed with leather-bound tomes, scroll cases of ivory and onyx, and ancient tablets. Shriveled specimens hunched in jars. The room was dirty and unkempt. The urn perched upon an altar in the center of the room. Odd glyphs were painted upon the floor. Several eunuchs stood silently against the walls.

Dmitri looked ghostly and sinister in the flickering torchlight. "You must understand that we are worms compared to the grandeur that lurks beyond the stars." He swatted a gnat. "Great beings beyond time and space once ruled this planet, millions of years ago. They have slumbered through the eons, awaiting men such as myself who are learned in the esotery of their summoning." Half a smile crept across Dmitri's face. "They yearn to awaken from their slumber and rule the stars once again." He dragged a finger across the lid of the urn and said, "I know that I promised you wealth, but I plan to give you something far more valuable than gold." A malignant smile split his face and he pried the lid from the container.

Jarvos heard the eunuchs mutter. "You're going to end up like the rest of those maggoty priests, Dmitri."

Dmitri smiled. "Hardly. I have spent my whole life studying and researching and preparing for this. The difference between those dreadful priests is that they worship beings such as Jun-Nabbath." Dmitri wove his spider fingers together and said: "I have no desire to grovel and supplicate it. I wish to learn from it. I will to unleash it and harness its immense power and use it to reshape the world to my own liking." Dmitri smiled. "With the power of Jun-Nabbath, I will crush my enemies and fashion for myself a crown made of stars. The civilized nations of the world will grovel and lick my feet."

Dmitri clutched a scroll that looked as though it had been rendered from human flesh and began to recite the verses that were etched upon it. He spoke in a language that Jarvos had never heard before. His voice descended several octaves as his mouth and throat uttered profane sounds. Jarvos saw Gaunt thrash like a fish and free one of his arms. Then the torches flickered and an indescribably foul smell filled the room. Jarvos retched and he heard the eunuchs gag and mutter to one another. Their own imprecations formed a sort of counterpoint to the awful melody that Dmitri recited.

Jarvos's skin erupted in gooseflesh as a shadow spilled from the urn and dripped putrescence onto the floor. It was coaxed and goaded by Dmitri's chanting. Its pale bulk rose ten feet, then twenty feet, then thirty. Its head brushed the rafters of the tower ceiling and it continued to uncoil from the urn – one segment at a time. Jarvos knew that it would continue to grow, just as the mural in the tower had depicted. Jun-Nabbath would burst through the roof and continue to rise until it curled around the moon and strangled it. What then?

Jarvos felt his bladder give and a pool of urine spread beneath him. Several of the eunuchs screamed. Two of them sank to the ground and shivered in their excrement, drooling and gibbering. Another jumped from the window and shattered the roof of the arboretum.

Dmitri continued to chant, undisturbed. Ink bled from his eyes as he looked up at the thing that had slumbered in that urn. The scroll undulated behind him in waves of dried skin; he clutched it so hard that his nails tore into the parchment on which the verses had been written. Jarvos was so petrified that he couldn't blink. His throat closed off his screams. He feared that his heart would stop as Jun-Nabbath's shadow curled across the room. He prayed that death would take him before that horrid thing swallowed him, kicking and screaming. He felt his innards turn to jelly as the chant continued on. He watched Dmitri's mouth writhe as the ancient words scraped from his throat. He considered attempting to swallow his tongue when he noticed one of the eunuchs slip behind Dmitri. It was the same eunuch that Dmitri had punched in the parlor; his lips parted in a snarl as he drew a gold dagger from his loincloth and buried it in Dmitri's back, again and again. Dmitri screamed and fell onto his stomach. He lay still for a moment, and then he picked up the scroll and attempted to begin the ritual from where he'd left off, but he'd lost his place. The eunuch grabbed him by the hair and sliced open his throat. Blood poured through Dmitri's fingers as he clutched the altar and pulled himself to his feet.

He looked up at Jun-Nabbath and seemed to plead with the ancient beast. Jun-Nabbath's mouth split and revealed teeth the size of spears; a dozen tongues spewed from its mouth as it bellowed with such ferocity that the rafters shook and the tower threatened to topple. Jarvos covered his ears and screamed when the beast crashed down upon Dmitri and grasped him in its massive jaws. Its head shattered the stone wall of the tower as it thrashed about. Then it snapped Dmitri in half as it reared one last time and sunk back into the urn. Jarvos cackled while the eunuch severed the ropes which bound him. His laughter degenerated into howls and continued until Gaunt was free and his friend dragged him to his feet and smacked him. They stumbled over one another as they fled through the doorway and descended a spiral staircase.

***

Jarvos rested his forearms on the railing of the sailing vessel Ghost and stared at the grey waters of the Bleak Sea. "It will be good to spend some time in Aquilas."

Gaunt gulped wine from a skin. "I hear war is brewing in the southern duchies. I'll probably try to find a mercenary company headed south. I know The Broken Blades are still roaming about. Perhaps they'll take me back."

"I think I'm done with war," said Jarvos.

"You're full of it." Gaunt handed him the wineskin. "Once you're out in the field for a few months and you've been around some camp followers, you'll realize how much you've missed it."

"We still haven't talked about what happened," Jarvos wiped wine from his lips.

"What is there to talk about?" Gaunt snatched the wine skin and emptied it down his throat. "I still think we had some bad lotus and we hallucinated."

Jarvos smiled, "No you don't, Gaunt."

"Well, all the same, I'm tired of the nightmares." He threw the wineskin overboard. "I hope I never see that wretched city as long as I live."

"And you believe that you'll stop dreaming in Aquilas?"

"No," said Gaunt, "But the streets are clean and the whores wash themselves once in a while."

"I can't think of whores or any other diversions, now that I've seen what I saw," said Jarvos.

They both stared at the cold, grey waters for quite some time. Jarvos looked up at the stars and thought of the things that slumbered eternally in the hidden reaches of the world - gods without name, all but forgotten save for a few perverse souls foolish enough to believe that they can control such monstrosities; it was enough to make him tear out his hair and throw himself in the frigid waters. He looked down at the sack that was next to his boot. "It took every ounce of courage to return to Dmitri's tower and retrieve that thing. I don't even want to look at it."

"You just wanted to see if the eunuchs forgot anything when they looted Dmitri's manse." Gaunt's smile melted when he placed the urn on the railing of the vessel and stared at it.

Fear slithered through the Red Islander's guts. "Get rid of it."

"There isn't an ocean deep enough." Gaunt threw it with all his might and they watched it sink beneath the waves.

FATE UNKIND

TIMOTHY P. REMP

Sir Andromalius swayed back and forth on his warhorse as he traversed an old forest. He closed his eyes and tilted back his head. Behind his punished dark eyes were those who died by his faery sword, Mal'Rapture. A light rain caressed his face, matted his hair. He pulled off a gauntlet and ran his hand over his head. He held his palm before him, mesmerized by bloody channels accenting his long lifeline. Diluted droplets speckled the muddy earth.

Since his encounter with a faery sword-bearer, he left nothing behind but a wake of blood and death. The blade's savage hacking of the fallen fed his euphoria, frightening and enthralling him all at once. He chanted to himself all in the name of my lord's justice.

He pulled Mal'Rapture from its scabbard and held it before him. The sword was carved from a single piece of frosted crystal. A blooming rose adorned the sword's rain-guard; obsidian vines and twisted thorns marked its cross-guard. A single tear-dropped diamond crowned the pommel.

"What do you want from me," he whispered to the blade. Rain drops dripped silently off its point.

He looked up and recognized a few trees from his youth. Have I traveled back so far? he thought.

He sheathed Mal'Rapture, gathered the reins and said, "I know the way."

Andromalius guided his steed over old roots and ancient trees until the forest thinned and opened onto a grassy field. A familiar old hut squatted in the center of the field.

He hesitated outside. The scent of herbs and dried meats educed childhood memories. He stared at the entrance, heard her toneless hum. After a deep breath, he tore the animal skins aside and entered.

"Mother, I'm home."

A sagging fireplace dominated one side of the interior; musty bedding filled the opposite space below a fur-covered wall. In the center, an old woman in tattered robes hunched over a rough wooden table. She cut raw vegetables and tossed them into a caldron etched with a witch's pentagram. She mumbled to herself without looking up.

"Mother. It's me."

She kept cutting.

"Mother?"

She stopped.

"It's your son."

She lifted her wizened head to stare at him with feeble eyes. "My son is dead." She laid the knife down and wiped her hands.

"I am not dead."

She reached for the caldron but Andromalius placed his gauntlet-covered hand over her gnarled ones.

"I'm right here with you, Mother."

She pulled away. "My little boy left me a long time ago."

"I came back. I need you to tell me about this." He touched the tear-dropped diamond pommel of his faerie blade.

She brushed strands of hair away from her eyes. "Your knight's sword will always serve you well. The other..." She pointed at Mal'Rapture.

"Yes..."

"I see only death."

"Death? Is it my death?"

She struggled with the caldron, shouldered her son out of the way and hung it over the cooking fire.

Andromalius grasped her shoulders and spun her around. "Answer me mother! Use your second sight. Look beyond the veil."

"Will it reveal my boy?" She sat heavily in an old wicker chair; a small wooden mug shook on a tiny table next to her. From the folds of her robes, she withdrew a pinch of powder and tossed it into the mug, swirled it and then took a drink. She closed her eyes and licked her lips. Her breathing slowed.

In a husky voice, she said, "Mal'Rapture blesses you with power... and curses you to slay the ones you love. You will always be alone."

Andromalius drew the crystal blade. Firelight danced along its edges. She looked at Andromalius, then the blade and gave a feeble smile.

"I love you, son."

The sword grew heavy in his hand. He tilted the blade forward and red liquid flowed though its mercurial channel. He looked from the blade to her and felt... nothing. He sheathed the blade and left the hut. The wavering skins deadened her stifled sobs.

He never heard goodbye.

AS ABOVE

TOBIAS LOC

Ahotain the Sorcereress shared her power with her twin brother Klaeth, for in the beginning, she had created the Dark of the Moon, and he the Bright Moon. Though they both held high positions within the court of Haelel Ahn, Ahotain longed to be queen with a desire that burned within her night and day, and gave her no rest.

She dared not challenge the king to ritual combat, for her magick waxed and waned with the phases of the Moon. If she struck while at the height of her power, her enemies at court would simply wait until she was helpless to challenge her.

Ahotain's unfulfilled desire was slowly choking the life from her body. She grew desperate, finding inspiration in the delirium and ecstasy of the black lotus — most deadly of plants. If she could trick her brother into revealing his True Name, she could steal his power and never again feel her shameful weakness.

Klaeth loved only two things in the entire world: his sister and his wine. Ahotain rarely indulged because she had no taste for the juice of the grape, but now she went to her brother bearing his favorite vintage. In a hidden vial she carried a distillation of black lotus, meant to confound his will and compel him to speak truly. They talked and drank for long hours before Klaeth became distracted long enough for her to poison his wine. The potent virtue in the plant unhinged Klaeth's mind and he ran screaming into the street. There he met his death under the hooves of a team of horses and the wheels of a chariot.

When the shade rose from his lifeless body, it was filled with pain and the weight of betrayal. Though he tried to rise to the heavens, the weight of his misery bore him back down to the earth. Drawing strength from his True Name, he arose and flew to the Moon. There he swore an oath that bound his soul in chains.

The Demon of the Moon turned from his eternal vigil to gaze upon the Upper Dark. The Children of Onaul moved above him ceaselessly, watching Ilder'en with dead and hungry eyes. Beyond them, his brothers and sisters blazed with celestial glory. At the furthest limit of his senses, Klaeth could hear the Maelstrom, a sea at war with the heavens, a raging battle that never ceased.

Then he heard the music. It began as a distant reverberation, a long dead echo that promised him things he did not understand. Klaeth rose to follow the sound, but the iron chains binding his limbs held fast. The music grew louder. A god taking the universe and beating upon it like a drum could not compare to the wild abandon and the elemental fury of that sound.

Words spoken in madness two centuries ago echoed again in his mind. I vow to hold vigil until the world has crumbled into dust or I understand why my beloved sister murdered me. He strained against his bonds until they tore into his skin and blood fell upon the ground, where it joined the pool of sweat his efforts had caused him to shed.

At last he collapsed and lay still. The music had grown distant and his strength was spent. With the last of his will, he lifted his face and addressed the sound itself. "Are you god or demon? Whither do you come and whom do you serve?"

"I am god and I am demon." the music answered. "I am the sorrow within my lady's heart when the Word came upon her, and I serve her child even as his children pay service unto me."

Klaeth looked again upon the Upper Dark. The seven Archons had ceased their endless prowling between the stars. A crack appeared in space, a jagged hole that burned with spectral light. One by one they drifted toward the scar, black wings beating a slow, reluctant rhythm. The Children of Onaul vanished and the crack closed behind them.

"I name thee Lohuth Ennka. Thou art the Aeon of Incorruptible Will, for none other could have commanded those horrors as you have done." he said.

"And I commend a dead drunkard upon his obvious learning in the sacred arts," replied Ennka. "Follow and learn of greater mysteries."

"How am I to follow bound in chains?"

"Only thy soul is bound. Leave it and follow if you would learn true knowledge."

"Let the damn thing rot. I am sick of it. Take me where you will..."

***

I arose from my prison and looked with eyes unclouded. Light and darkness, the two moved upon the surface of the moon as oil moves upon water. The moon is water. Every grain of dust held the roar and crash of mighty waves, waves crested with flame. A sea ablaze and burning with the glory of the sun.

I looked down upon my soul and hoped that it would die quickly. Ennka stood before me now, a woman etched in starlight. Red hair flowed about her, a mane that moved as if blown by an unseen zephyr. She wore a brown dress and an unadorned circlet of gold. Her face was plain, but handsome. The eyes were the exception; Ennka had eyes that could shatter iron. They had looked upon the inferno of creation and the utter desolation of infinite space, and been unmoved to tears.

"The Seven wait and watch," she said, "They bind the light within dense matter and dull the minds of men. They are the first guardians on the path, but we shall pass their station unmolested."

My companion led me upward into the celestial vault. Below I beheld Ilder'en in its entirety. Not round as some philosophers guessed, but flat and unending in all direction. A few thousand islands scattered over an azure sea that faded into a haze at the limits of my vision. The sun descended towards a blackened and glassy isle and the waters boiled for miles around. White vapor rose; when it cleared, the sun had gone, swallowed by the earth where the great serpents and dead gods would rend it and devour its burning flesh. The sun would wander in the dark, its life pouring forth from uncounted wounds until the priests of Ilder'en ransomed it back with the blood of sacred oxen and the wailing cries of the faithful.

"I have heard the voices of the stars. They are ever filled with a sadness I fail to understand. Do they weep for themselves or for all mankind?" I asked.

"They weep as they ever have, for the death of formlessness and the pain of separation."

"And what of the end of the path? To what do we aspire?"

"Only to that which is bornless and boundless, unnamed and unnamable. All else is naught but illusion and shadow-play."

"Is that where we are destined?"

"Thou art unworthy of that sight. A single glance would shatter thee."

The stars moved about us now and at the heart of each, a god stood silhouetted in brilliant white fire. It shone through their skin and illuminated the night sky. The Maelstrom roared loudly now, close but still unseen.

"Why did she poison the wine?" I shouted, finally giving words to the suffering that had chained me.

Ennka turned and met my gaze with her deadly eyes. Kingdoms fell into dust below us, and others arose while she looked within me. Then she smiled and turned away, dissolving into light and shadow as she turned. "I am needed Above."

And she was gone.

***

Slowly I fell. Past the eternal stars. Past the tomb of my soul, waning now, looking down upon a world painted bright with autumn. The morning sun, bleeding crimson light from countless wounds, tore itself free from the earth and rose anew.

The island of my birth appeared below me. The kingdoms and baronies of the Mortal-Gods stood upon the banks of a great river valley, sheltered from the desert by the mountains on either side. The royal palace stood as it had during my lifetime, though now it was crowned with spires of silver and brass.

A half remembered instinct drew me south-east, over the Irit mountain range and along the edge of the Azhail desert. The black sand stretched to the horizon, broken only by the bleached bones of camels and men. A solitary caravan carried upon the shoulders of fifty slaves trudged its way toward the mountains. The caravan's one remaining wheel dangled uselessly from its axle.

I continued my flight and reached the last mountain before the sea. At its base, the Blue Pillars stood as if frozen in a swaying spiral dance. Each pillar was a single shard of crystal twice the size of a grown man. Sigils and bind-runes and barbarous words of power had been etched into their surface millennia ago.

My murderer knelt among the stones, arms crossed over her chest and head bowed in supplication. It was only then that I felt the power of the Dark Moon, coiling through her prayers and into the blue stones. Reaching out with dead, unseen hands to grasp me and draw me in.

I had never trained in the sorcerous arts as my sister had, preferring the easy life of a gentleman. I did not know what words or rites would loose the fleshless hands that bound me. But I had learned secrets on the Moon. I had heard the Demons of the Upper Dark whisper blasphemies to each other and I had caught glimpses of the dreams of gods.

As I stumbled towards the stone circle, I threw my right arm over my eyes and etched a symbol in the air with my left hand. The symbol blazed with black light, an inferno raging in my outstretched hand. I had conjured the Sign of Alkemneth, a sacred mystery of High Magick, and I dared not look upon what I had wrought. I felt it grow tendrils of light, felt it writhe in my grasp like a baby squid plucked from the depths. As it sank sharp hooks into my forearm, I gasped out its True Name and the words that bind it.

"DATHAEN ANUUL! Athay! Klo! Fuethark!"

I felt my blood course through the devil on my arm. Slow, inhuman thoughts circled in the deep places of my mind, and then we joined. I opened my eyes and saw the world's true face. Regret and black despair covered my sister like a shroud. The music of the spheres echoed through the blue crystals. Discordant notes tainted it and malignant power hid in the silences.

I lashed out with my tentacles, wrapping them around the fleshless hands that drew me towards an uncertain fate at the heart of the stone circle. I squeezed with a dozen limbs and felt bones snap under the pressure. Ahotain recoiled as her sorcery collapsed. She turned and looked into my eyes.

She looked broken. Her face was thin and haggard; her eyes dull with lotus smoke. She stroked the sides of a long-stemmed pipe with her fingers as she stared at me.

"Forgive?" Her voice was cracked with age. "Forgive me?"

"Tell me why?" I strode forward and the grass beneath my feet blackened and died. "Why?" The tendrils fell upon her like a dozen lashes. She cried as the barbs tore her flesh. "Tell me!" I lifted my hand to strike again.

She threw up her arms to shield herself and shrieked a curse, "Arsh ren Armet ash Ihl Aze-Ka!" Twin lightning bolts struck the central pillar as she spoke and the report blasted me off my feet. I watched in a daze as the pillar began to bleed from its wound. The ruby liquid formed a pool around its base. From this pool, wet and covered with blood, a monstrous creature clawed its way into reality. The Aze-Ka had a dragon's head, the body of a great cat, and the legs and translucent tail of a moon lizard. Fiery venom fell from its angular maw in rivulets.

Then as I struggled to stand it spoke in a voice that resounded from within the very earth: "Ahotain, daughter of Dradin, by what right hast thou called me forth?"

"I call thee forth by the dread name Ilzesisthur and by the Chains of Fire. By YAVAY, Herald of the Most High and by Sabbious the Mouth of the Abyss! Obey me or thou shalt suffer all the torments of fire and crushing earth and every foul wind and plague shall descend upon thee."

The Aze-Ka smiled a wolfish smile, "I might happily kill thee and desecrate thy corpse O daughter of Dradin, for the affront thou hast given me. I stay my hand only for the sake of thy noble father and the accord he struck with me. Charge me and be done!"

"I charge thee to destroy my brother's spirit."

The beast turned and the weight of its gaze crushed me, holding me helpless to the ground. We fought, my devil and I. We struggled to break the will of the god that bound us. The Aze-Ka took a step nearer and then another. As it loomed over me, letting its venom drip into my eyes, I felt a searing pain in my left arm and know that my devil had fled like a rat from a sinking ship.

I gathered my strength. The despair of two centuries and the inhuman beauty of Ennka flooded my mind as I sharpened my will and hurled it against the Aze-Ka. In a fit of triumphant ecstasy, I screamed a word that even the gods are forbidden to speak. The word struck the beast like a hammer blow and it staggered back. A wound opened upon its chest, burning and boiling with black ichor. Fear flashed in its eyes, and then it saw that my strength was broken and it smiled. Golden teeth closed on my neck and I died the second death.

"Thy father's soul tasted far sweeter than thy brother. Farewell...."
The Aze-Ka embraced the nearest crystal pillar and faded away into its depths. The girl lay on her side, crying silently, she had snapped her pipe in half and it lay broken on the grass.

***

My pseudopods and tentacles burn where the venom splashed them. I slither from my hiding place, feeling the stolen strength course through me as I creep up the mountainside. The twice dead sorcerer made a poor vessel. No mortal vices to indulge. No strong mortal hands with which to snap an innocent neck. I crawl inside the girl and see the cracks that run through her mind. Deep fissures where madness lurks. I reach into the oldest scar and tare it open. Her mind shatters around me and I feast on her memories, her passions and lusts.

Once I am sated, I catch a glimpse of her most secret and burning desire and I smile to myself. I sit up in my new body, and then I stand and begin walking towards the Valley of the Mortal-Gods. When the King lays broken at my feet, I will claim the throne and the Blood-Red Sword will be mine to command.

GOD OF THE CATACOMBS

TREY CAUSEY

Through the absolute dark of the catacombs they came.

Tentative, furtive, but growing bolder, the things crept toward him. There were four, five perhaps. They approached on bare feet whose quiet padding was accompanied with tiny clicks from nails or claws. They whispered to each other in gurgling tones, sounds that seemed to mock language, but unmistakably had meaning.

Zakoji sat with his back against the strangely smooth tiles of the wall, his legs crossed, his hands cupped in his lap. His dark hair, unbound, hung over his eyes. Except for his slow, steady breathing, he was motionless. If the catacomb denizens sensed him somehow through the darkness—and he was sure that they did—they must have thought him sleeping.

In this, they erred. Zakoji was deep in a warrior's trance. His body rested, but his senses were sharp. He heard their movements in the tomblike stillness, but more than that he felt them. Their cold, clammy life-essence seemed almost to assail him. The closer they came, the more loathsome it was.

Their wariness began to give way. They were almost close enough now to touch him. They had a musty odor like the cast off skin of a snake, but Zakoji sensed that they were vaguely manlike, almost human. Or once human.

Now they were certainly close enough to touch him, but they hesitated. He could almost feel them trembling in the darkness. Whether it was from

fear, or anticipation, he couldn't judge. Did they see his sword—the sword of his father and his father's father—sheathed and lying next to him? If so, did they understand its meaning?

One of them shifted and let out a soft moan. It was going to touch him, or worse. Zakoji didn't wait to find out. Quicker than the thing's reaching hand, Zakoji had grasped his sword, pulled it from its sheath, and lashed out at the dark.

The things gave wet squeals of surprise. They were quicker than Zakoji had imagined. They cringed back, and his blade cut only the dank air.

Zakoji leapt to his feet. He assumed the stance that began the sword-form "Willow in the Gale"—the form most masters agreed was best for fighting blind—and braced himself for the things' attack. When studying them, he had never thought he would have to put the esoteric dissertations of those sword scrolls into practice.

The effort was wasted. The things loped back into the darkness, some braying, others hissing what Zakoji surmised must pass for curses among their kind. Soon their sounds were no louder than the beating of his own heart in his ears. Then they were gone all together.

Zakoji reached down and found his scabbard. He sheathed his sword, and then stuck it under his belt sash. He stood alone in the darkness.

Time to move on.

This was the second encounter he had had since entering the catacombs. He had no wish to have a third. The first had cost him his last torch. He had slain a bloated, pale creature the size of a horse he would have sworn was a gigantic grub, if not for its fetid breath and the warmth of the black blood he had cleaned from his blade afterward. The second encounter had only ended his restorative meditation prematurely. It could undoubtedly get worse.

He found the wall with his left hand. The tunnels, more than wide enough for three men to walk abreast, were almost completely circular. The walls were covered in black tiles. They were uncannily smooth under his fingers, almost as if they were oiled. The gaps between them were so tight and uniform they reminded Zakoji of the scales of a snake.

"Keep to the main tunnel. Enter none of the smaller branches." The monks had told him. "Move as quick as you can. Don't tarry." The wisdom of some of their advice had been borne out. The proof of the rest would be seen in time.

He reached into the pouch he carried. He had only one candle left for light. With flint, steel, and the tinder he carried, he lit it with practiced ease despite the darkness. Its glow was yellowed and weak, but it was the center of Zakoji's world at the moment. At best, the candle wouldn't last long, but the monks had told him it was only a day's walk through the tunnel at a good pace. Time was a strange thing in the darkness, but Zakoji would stake his oath that the better part of a day had passed already. He must be near the way out. He had to be.

One hand on the wall to guide him, Zakoji continued his march through the tunnel. He hoped he moved toward the outside world.

He silently cursed the Celestial Minister of Fates and whatever lesser heavenly bureaucrats were the architects of his current predicament. If only events hadn't forced him to leave the Imperial port of Tseroku with such haste. How the eyes of the Empire had found him he couldn't say, but they had. Even in the thick, fish-smelling fogs of the northern Imperial frontier, the Empress could make her displeasure known.

The latest assassin was a smirking young noble, Nenuri na Takume Jichiro. He had challenged Zakoji by his old name—the name Zakoji had surrendered when he had betrayed duty and caste. The name of a man the Empress had ordered to commit ritual suicide as the price of disobedience.

This Jichiro was little more than a boy. He was about the same age Zakoji had been when he had knelt and been made a paladin of the young Empress, whose throne name was Precious Star of Dawn. Jichiro wore the imperial heron crest in gold on his surcoat, as well. He too was a paladin; his head was filled with boyish notions of honor and duty.

They had stood in the muddy street, facing each other; Jichiro with his fine silks shielded by an oiled-paper raincoat, and his hair fixed in a warrior's topknot, faced Zakoji, unshaven and in worn clothes, unruly strands of hair plastered to his face by the damp, sea air.

Before their swords were drawn, Zakoji had perceived something else. The Empress had taken the young paladin as a lover. He saw it in Jichiro's eyes. As the duel was joined, Zakoji fancied he could almost smell her perfume on the swaggering youth—a scent made for her and her alone.

He had felt no jealousy when he killed the paladin, he told himself. The young woman he had known had ceased to be when she had ascended the Jade Dragon Throne. He had no right to question an Empress on what lovers she might take, what lives she might use.

Zakoji had wiped a paladin's blood from his blade with a piece of rice paper, as he pushed the girl—now an empress—from his mind. After he had said a quick prayer for the dead man, he had his thoughts to escape from Tseroku, and the Empire, as quickly as possible.

The gods had favored him in that, at least—or so he thought at the time. Escape had come in the form of employment as a bodyguard on a Thuleslanic League trading mission led by an ambitious merchant called Bald Hraethno.

Hraethno led them northward across the Frozen Sea on ice-ships sailed on steel runners edged with crystalline adamant. Their destination was a broad, wind-swept mesa on the far shore. On and inside that mesa was a relic of a lost age, the lamasery-city of Ghothrune. It was in this forbidding and ill-omened place that Hraethno hoped to make the fortune that would elevate him to the position of syndic, maybe even optimate, in the League.

He now lay dead on a basalt slab in the bowels of Ghothrune. The merchant had taken ill on the ships to the mesa, and the diet of fungi and tubers grown in the grotto-gardens underneath the city had not been enough to keep him from wasting away. In less than ten days after their arrival, Hraethno was dead and Zakoji was without an employer.

Hraethno's death was more than poor diet, Zakoji was sure. There was something oppressive in the air of Ghothrune; a wrongness. He could feel it in the corpse-pale, blue light given off by the ancient crystal orbs in the corridors, and in the dreamy detachment of its monks and townsfolk. When the yellow veiled and turbaned High Lama had appeared before them and stood in silence while the attendant who spoke for him informed them of Hraethno's passing, Zakoji had decided he would leave the city and return to the ships.

The other Thuleslani could not be convinced. They were a fatalistic, superstitious people, over-concerned with omens and portents. The death of Hraethno and the oppressive strangeness of Ghothrune had convinced them that their grim gods had marked them. Some began practicing their death-songs; others fingered fetishes and talismans, and prayed.

Better to die in warmth among their fellows than in the ice and snow, where a man's soul could be forever lost. The Thuleslani were northmen, and they knew all too well the hazards of the blizzard that had howled around the mesa since their arrival. To take the narrow path down from city to seashore now would be certain death.

In this Zakoji agreed. He had another route in mind. They had all noticed the heavy, barred doors in parts of the city, which were often posted with armed guards. When Zakoji had asked a tailor with whom he had done business about them, he was told that these were entrances to the catacombs, tunnels older than the city itself. No one had ventured into the tunnels in a generation, but the tailor averred that one of the tunnels led to the base of the mesa.

"Why are the doors guarded?" Zakoji had asked.

"Ah, that," the tailor had replied in the languid way of the Ghothrune-folk. "Because there are things in the catacombs best left in the darkness. They emerge sometimes, these monsters..."

Zakoji understood. The doors were not barred to keep the people of Ghothrune out of the catacombs, but to keep their denizens in.

The Thuleslani had still refused to go. They scratched their pattern-tattooed chins in mock contemplation, and consulted what meager means of divination they had at their disposal. They decided the signs said they would die if they went. The truth, Zakoji suspected, was that the strange lassitude that afflicted the people of Ghothrune had begun to affect them as well.

He vowed he wouldn't succumb to such a fate. If Heaven willed that he brave ancient tunnels and subterranean creatures to escape it, then so be it. He was Zakoji of the warrior caste of Tsann, and a former paladin of the Empress, herself, after all.

Zakoji gathered a few supplies then got directions from one of the monks as to which entrance to take. With light, a steady pace, and luck, a man could make it in a day. He would come through the path to a cave whose mouth practically overlooked the place where the ships had docked.

With light, a steady pace, and luck.

Those had proved more elusive than Zakoji had foreseen. He had lost his light, and there were dangers abiding in the dark.

It would avail him little to waste further thought on his fate. He walked on, moving as quickly as he could without hurling himself blindly into the unknown. Occasionally, he would see brief flashes like tiny will-o'-wisps dart in front of him. He decided that this was merely his mind playing tricks—responding to his eyes' hunger for light.

The darkness outside the small light of his candle was more than total; it was almost palpable. It seemed to squeeze in on him, try to envelop him. He quickened his step as much as he dared, trying to outpace the sensation.

Lost in his thoughts, it perhaps took him longer than it might have to notice the sound of footsteps trailing him. The sound was not like the gentle rasping of his fur boots, nor the four-footed padding of some animal. It sounded like the bare feet of the things that approached him earlier, the catacomb-dwellers.

Zakoji again quickened his pace. Better to outdistance them than face them in the dark tunnels they called home. Intent on the footfalls behind him, he only too late noticed the scratching above him.

There was a throaty cry that made Zakoji's skin crawl. One of the dwellers dropped from the ceiling above him. Zakoji fell to floor under the thing's assault. He dropped his candle and it rolled, still lit, through a circular doorway on the left side of the tunnel. The thing's breath was hot and damp on his cheek, and smelled of rot. Zakoji yanked his sword from his sash, and brought it up between them, so that its pommel struck the thing under the chin. At the same time, Zakoji twisted his body and threw the thing off him.

It struck the tunnel wall, but was quickly on its feet. It lunged again, braying wetly.

Zakoji's sword slash caught it across the middle in mid-lunge. Its noise died abruptly in its throat, and it fell away, all but cleaved in two.

Zakoji felt for the open passageway then stepped through. The candle still burned, barely, on the ground in front of him. He would've snatched it up, if he hadn't been forced to turn and face the charge of a group of the catacomb-dwellers.

He ducked the leap of the first, slashing it from throat to groin as it passed over him. This motion flowed easily into cutting the throat of the next. In its haste the third impaled itself on Zakoji's blade, its long-fingered, grimy-nailed hands reached for his face, even as its death rattle left its throat.

Three died, but more followed. There were ten or more, pressed so close and attacking so suddenly Zakoji couldn't count them. With his blade not yet freed, the things overran him, and the weight of wiry bodies pushed him to the floor. Their fall blew the candle out and the dark engulfed them all.

Zakoji fought them hand to hand. Their skin was like an eel's. Their bodies seemed all sinew and muscle, as if their bones were less solid than normal creatures. Their clawing hands were relentless; their stinking maws snapped at him from everywhere in the darkness.

Neither Zakoji nor his foes noticed the dark soften from an absolute black to a gray-brown. They didn't see the ghostly radiance become a thing unto itself—an anemic blue glow spreading across the room. Zakoji did finally take notice when a pinprick of pale light emerged in the doorway, like a wound in the body of the dark.

The catacomb-dwellers took notice too, though by nonhuman means, as they were completely sightless. The bulges where their eyes would be were grown over by pasty, gray skin. They sensed it somehow, that was certain. They moaned and cringed from the approaching light like it was the sun, itself, come into their tunnels.

They slunk away to the walls of the room, clawing at them, trying to find some way to escape the light as it came ever closer. It moved from the threshold into the room. Its source was a globe, held high.

The light, though really only a pale glow, stung Zakoji's eyes as well, accustomed as they had become to darkness. He was able to make out that a human, and unmistakably feminine, silhouette held the globe aloft.

The bearer of the globe spoke in tones of command. The words were strange and like no human language Zakoji had ever heard. Its effect on the catacomb-dwellers was instantaneous. They fell almost in unison to their knees, tortured moans warbling in their throats.

Again the woman bearing the light spoke. Cringing, crawling, the things withdrew from the room back into the tunnels. In moments, even their plaintive sounds had faded into the darkness beyond the blue light's reach.

As the catacomb-dwellers retreated, Zakoji got to his feet. He pulled his sword from the body of one of the creatures. He flicked the blood from his blade then resheathed it. He did these things, and he watched the woman approach.

Strange how she didn't seem to traverse all the distance between where she first stood and where she finally stood in front of him. Close enough to touch him. She was slight, but well formed, and unmistakably so, in her sheer gown that left one shoulder bare. The gown and the body that wore it were both white and completely unblemished as far as Zakoji could tell in the blue glow. But the gown was hazy, like congealed mist, while the woman's skin was like fine porcelain.

Her eyes, larger than human and almost cat-like, looked up at him. They were a blue as pale as the Frozen Sea, a blue as pale as the light she carried. She smiled.

"Who are you?" Zakoji asked.

"I am of the catacombs." She answered in the tongue of the Empire, without a trace of an accent. She was undeniably beautiful, but there was a quality to that beauty Zakoji couldn't give name that unsettled as much as it pleased.

Zakoji's face must have given away some hint of his unease, because the woman said, "There are more dwelling in these tunnels than the degenerate creatures that attacked you. We find this ancient place a better home than the frozen top of the mesa."

Zakoji gave her a curt nod of acknowledgement. "The way out of these tunnels...is it far?"

"No, warrior," she said. "Not far. I will take you, but you should tend your wound first."

She gestured to his left arm. Zakoji lifted it to examine it in the pale light. There was a bleeding cut along his forearm he hadn't noticed. It wasn't deep, but Zakoji had seen wounds just as superficial fester and poison the man who bore them without the proper attention.

"Sit," the woman said. "Rest a moment and treat the wound. The creatures will not return soon."

The woman knelt on the stone and the placed the orb next to her. She looked up at Zakoji, expectantly.

Zakoji sat down, cross-legged, on the other side of the light globe. Now that his eyes were more adjusted to the light, he could see that it was a crystalline sphere half-full with a viscous, translucent, pale blue liquid. It was this liquid that was luminescent. Zakoji was sure that it was the source of the lighting within the lamasery above, as well. The odd color of the light was the same.

He found the bottom edge of his silk under-robe. After cutting the hem with his knife, he tore off two strips of cloth. The first he used to clean away the blood and dirt from his forearm.

The woman watched him with an expression he couldn't read. "You are a warrior of Tsann?" she asked, her tone amused. "A knight out of the epics?"

Zakoji was unsure if she mocked him, but he answered nonetheless. "I was born of the warrior caste, but I am no knight. I am wood adrift on the waves; a leaf borne by the wind."

"A masterless knight-errant, then," she said.

Zakoji didn't reply. He took the second strip of silk and bound his wound. Then, he flexed and extended his arm until he satisfied himself that the bandage would hold.

When that was done, he said to the women, "Your knowledge of my homeland is surprising."

She laughed; it was a pleasant sound, out of place in its surroundings. "The outside world may have forgotten us, but we have not forgotten it."

Zakoji nodded. Though he didn't know why, he had the feeling the woman was deceiving him, or least holding something back.

"Your people," he asked. "Where are they?"

"We live in more hospitable branches of the catacombs," she said. "We seldom venture here, but when we learned of your presence, I was sent to guide you." She took the globe in her hand once again. "Tell me, warrior: why did you brave the catacombs alone?"

"The gods decide my fate, the same as any other man's," Zakoji said. "But even they can't make me sit passively to await it."

The woman regarded him for a moment then she rose gracefully to her feet. "Come. We should go now. The catacomb-dwellers should remain cowed, but it would wise not to test them."

Zakoji didn't get to his feet immediately. He didn't trust her. While she offered him escape, she could just as easily be leading him to his doom.

The woman stopped in the doorway and turned to look at him.

"Come." Her expression and tone bespoke impatience

Yet he had no choice. Her presence, or the light she carried, frightened the catacomb-dwellers. Without knowing which, he could scarcely take the light from her, even had he been willing to do so. Though the truth was far from pleasing, without her he was unprotected and lost in the dark.

Zakoji did the only thing he could. He got to his feet and followed.

They walked on in the blue light. How long they continued in the tunnels, Zakoji couldn't say. He had lost any reference for the passage of time. As they went he heard the gurgling cries of the catacomb-dwellers, the bellows of creatures similar to the grub-like thing he had slain, and several other bestial sounds he couldn't identify. It was as if their passing brought all the things of the darkness awake. Whether they were protesting the light, or paying it rude homage, Zakoji didn't know.

He put his hand on the hilt of his sword.

The woman must have noticed because in an amused tone, she said, "There is no need. We are in no danger."

"Do they always react this way when you pass?"

"The light," she said. "They recognize it."

They walked on. The tunnel seemed to take a small, but noticeable upward slope. Zakoji was heartened by this, small thing though it was.

After a time, they seemed to reach the tunnel's end. The wall in front of them was unlike any Zakoji had seen in the tunnels before. It was bare and rough-hewn, and had a gap running vertically in it.

"Here is your way out, warrior," the woman said. "This is a door that opens at the back of a cave at the base of the plateau."

Zakoji traced the seam in the wall with his hand. "How do I open it?"

The woman extended her hand holding the blue-lit globe. She spoke words in a guttural language that seem incongruous coming from her lips.

There was a sound like stone grinding against stone. After a moment, the gap between the stones began to widen, and it continued to widen until it was spread enough for a man to squeeze through sideways. Zakoji felt air blow through the new-made gap—cold, fresh, and briny.

"My thanks," Zakoji said. Wasting no time, he stepped toward the opening.

The woman stopped him with a hand on his arm. "Wait. You can't be sure how long you will search before you find others. Let me give you supplies."

Zakoji studied her. He read no treachery in her large, pale eyes, or in the slight smile on her thin lips.

"All right."

The woman gestured to another door to her left—a door where Zakoji was sure there had been only the tunnel wall before. Now the tiles seemed to have been spread apart in an alternating fashion around a vaguely diamond-shaped opening. They looked like black teeth in some alien maw.

"This is one of our storage rooms," the woman said. "You may take anything you need."

Zakoji hesitated. He still felt unsettled; but the woman had led him to the exit, and he would likely need provisions. Again, he decided he had to follow her. He stepped through the opening in the wall.

The room was larger than any he had seem in the catacombs. It was oval in shape and its walls were completely smooth. Not only were they unadorned, but there appeared to be no joints or seams where the stone had been fitted together. It was like a bubble, but one formed in rock. A narrow walkway rimmed a wide pit in the room's center. Emanating from the pit, beyond the obscuring edge of the walk, was a blue glow.

"What is this?" Zakoji asked. He thought he heard, faintly, but distinctly, a murmuring sound.

"Look for yourself." The woman said. "This is the reason we have come."

Zakoji stepped out onto the walk. The pit was filled with the glowing blue liquid, deep enough here so that it was opaque. Thick-walled bubbles, risen from unknown depths, periodically broke the luminescent smoothness of its surface. Now that he was closer, the murmuring was louder. It was like the distant sound of a crowd.

"This is the truth of the catacombs." The woman said from behind him. "Their heart. The reason for the catacombs and the monastery built above, though the fool monks have only a vague inkling of this. The ancestors of the catacomb-dwellers guessed more—and you've seen what that knowledge has wrought with them."

"It's alive," Zakoji said, quietly. He shook his head as if denying the truth of the realization.

The woman laughed. There was mockery in the sound. "It's a husk. A remnant."

"A husk?" Zakoji was barely listening. He strained to make out the words that rose on the blue light.

"It is the remnant of a god." The woman replied. "It is all that is left of one of those that began the world's creation in their glorious, terrible image. The usurper young gods...they razed true creation, and erected this callow mockery in its place."

There was a timbre of excitement in her voice, like she was on the verge of ecstasy.

"This is one of the Old Ones?" Tales Zakoji had learned from childhood made him recoil from the rim of the pit. From the priests tending the shrines of the Thrice-Million Gods, to itinerant monks of the Ascended One preaching on the roadside, the religions of the Empire warned of the Old Ones—the monstrous, inhuman, god-things that had been overthrown by the virtuous gods.

The gods had destroyed as many of their forebears as they could, and imprisoned or bound those they could not. They caused the captured Old Ones to re-dream the world into a place where they and their chosen followers, humanity, might prosper. The Old Ones were anathema to the world of man.

But there were always rumors. It was whispered that there remained humans and nonhumans that held to the Old Ones, and worshipped them in hidden rites for forbidden rewards.

There was a sound like a gong being struck. Ripples spread out across the surface of the liquid like it was a pond that a large stone had been thrown into.

Zakoji spun around to face the woman. He grasped the hilt of his sword. "Why did you bring me here, woman?" he snarled.

But the woman wasn't there.

"Its mindless now, this god-remnant." Her voice seemed to reverberate from the entire room, and it was different now, more like a chorus than a single voice. "Or more truthfully, its mind is made for a different world."

Zakoji scanned the room. The woman was nowhere to be seen. Warily, he moved toward the door.

"Can you imagine being cut off from all sensation?" The woman or chorus of women went on. The sound of the voices was becoming shrill. "It steals forms and sensations from the crude matter of this world, then fashions puppets of its own to experience the physicality

84

of our lives and deaths. All the things of the catacombs are its creations, its worshippers, or both. It hungers for experience. It must consume."

Zakoji's acute senses saved him. Just at the door, he spun around, and drew his sword in one fluid motion, executing perfectly the "Scythe at Reaping" sword-form. His blade slashed the woman who had appeared behind him across the throat.

The chorus of voices cried and shattered, becoming discordant. The blow should have cut her head from her neck. Instead her head only lolled, and luminescent, viscous, blue liquid oozed from her wound instead of blood.

The voices wailed. From the toppling body of the woman and from the pit, they wailed. But in the raw anger of the noise, Zakoji heard one word: desecration.

At the same time, the bubbling in the liquid grew louder. The remains of the Old One roiled against the sides of the pit. It was like a cauldron about to boil over.

Zakoji leaped through the opening in the wall. In the tunnel, he heard the sounds of the creatures of the darkness again, calling out in outrage or despair. They were coming closer. And he feared, so was the cacophonous sludge behind him.

But the narrow gap that he prayed led to the outside was still open. Without sparing another glance backward, he slid through the gap, followed by the cries of the shadow of a dead god and worshippers it had spawned.

Faint, white sunlight guided Zakoji to the mouth of the cave. He looked back from time to time to make sure he wasn't followed, but nothing emerged from the catacombs. He didn't know why, but he thanked the gods and the Ascended One for it, all the same.

As he stood at the cave's mouth, snow was falling, but the wind was gentle. Regardless, it was bitterly cold. Zakoji shivered, and pulled his cloak in tighter around him. Looking into the sky, he smiled.

The northern sky was gray and drear, but behind it, muted, was the pure light of the sun.

FROSTTOUCH

JAMES MACGEORGE

Ffnard was cold. Of all the myriad locations that Vayniris encompassed, of all the fabulous and awe inspiring places that its fabled far-gates could take him, he wished least of all to be in the one that would freeze the nipple from a witch's tit. Shifting his axe from one shoulder to the other, he snapped the leashes with his free hand, and the dogs leapt forward, pulling the sled back towards his encampment. He was anxious to be home before dark, but he spared a moment to look behind him. No sign of it, he thought with no small amount of relief..

The closer he came to his encampment, the more he relaxed. He allowed his mind to wander, just a bit. The last few weeks had been far from normal, but it was almost over.

***

As much as he hated to be out here in the Vorn-damned cold, he'd been making the trek every year without fail since he was old enough to hold the axe. First with his father, then by himself after his father had died. He'd been taught how to trap and skin enough prized albino beryaks in four weeks to keep his family sheltered and fed for a year. Next year, he'd likely bring his oldest, and begin teaching him how to trap.

The far-gate to this realm, long since forgotten by almost all, sat in a field behind the ramshackle home his family had held for generations. Every year at the same time, the stars would form the proper sequence and the far-gate would open. Ffnard would pack up his sled, rouse the dogs, and prepare for his trip, and each year his wife would do her best to stop him. Though they lived in an outlying borough of the Scattered City, they were no more than three far-gate jumps from the Market, and Vorn knew he couldn't sustain his brood without the income the pelts brought.

The far-gate itself was a prize, as it was much smaller than the typical gate, through which entire armies could march. While it was peculiar that this was a personal gate, made for just a single man, it was even stranger that it only opened for brief periods of time. Most far-gates were always open unless they had fallen into disrepair, and those typically did not operate at all.

The story of its discovery, as handed down through the generations, went that long ago, a member of his family had stumbled upon the gate while searching for a suitable place to bed the local blacksmith's daughter. Hidden in what was then a thick patch of woods, the suitor at first mistook it for the remnant of an ancient building, until he felt the cold, arctic air rushing through it. Curious, he ducked through its arch, telling the maiden to await his return. She did so, at first incensed, then worried, and finally frightened. Racing back to town, she gathered his brothers and, heavily armed, they stormed the frozen wasteland, only to find their wayward brother, gutted no more than twenty feet from the portal, a pure albino beryak lapping contentedly from a pool of spilled blood in the snow, bits of flesh between its teeth.

Beryaks, albino or otherwise, were dangerous to an individual but had a tendency to freeze up when presented with multiple opponents. While their sharp claws and teeth could open a body up with ease, their stubby legs, shambling gait, flat faces and front facing eyes made it difficult for them to defend themselves against more than one attacker. The brothers fell upon the beast with savage cries of vengeance. They skinned the corpse, brought its pelt back through the portal and hung it above their door, in accordance with their custom.

Over the following few days, several mourners remarked upon the pelt as they came to pay their respects, including a nobleman who, as it turned

out, was willing to pay an outrageous sum of money for it. He explained that there was a taboo amongst the nobles of Vayniris against harming or capturing live albino beryaks – supposedly, they were favored by some primordial god of the icy wastes, if you believed in that sort of thing.

A price was arranged, an agreement to supply more was struck, and so it was every year after that, when the stars were right and this peculiar little far-gate would open, someone in Ffnard's family would take their dogs out for four weeks. Four weeks was all they had, for at the end of those four weeks, the far-gate would shut again, not to open until the same time the following year.

Ffnard's family earned a steady living, and the nobles kept their precious hands clean. He snorted. He sure didn't mind trapping and skinning the hairy bastards, but then again, he was no noble. Grinning, he exposed his rotted teeth to the cold air, cleared his throat, and spat a warm brown slug of snot into the snow. The nobles might not want to kill the Vorn-damned things, but they didn't mind letting someone else kill them and then buying the skins as some sort of token of bravery.

He was tired of being cold, though - tired of the early rises, long days, and lonely nights with only a flickering flame and the whining of the dogs to keep him company. He was tired of wrapping himself in enough furs to survive the bitter cold and even more tired of taking them off at the end of the day.

One of his ancestors had built a shelter a half a day's ride from the far-gate; every year Ffnard planned to bring supplies with him to fix it up, but every year he left without them then spent every night of the four weeks cursing the drafty cabin and leaky roof. He missed his wife and her ample bosoms, his children and their careless laughter, the warm afternoons on his porch.

Just two more days, he thought. With over fifty pelts skinned and ready—more than he took in most years—he could leave now, but four weeks was four weeks, and he was only at three weeks and five days. The dogs were getting anxious, though, longing for the fat bellies and warm fires that were their reward year after year at the end of their trip into the cold. Each day they emerged from the makeshift kennel a little slower, looked at him just a little longer before accepting the harnesses, and whined a little louder at night after he'd put them up. They wanted to go home.

They weren't the only ones, he thought ruefully. His joints ached even more than they had the year before, and there wasn't a fire big enough to chase the ache away. Each morning he found himself thinking of the gate, thinking of the City beyond, thinking of home.

Four weeks was four weeks, he reminded himself. No matter how strange things had gotten.

***

This year's trip had begun well. Some years, it had taken him days to find a beryak, but this year he had found one on his first day. He tracked it back to its den, a shallow cave right on the side of a mountain he had traipsed up and down year after year, without ever seeing a single Vorn-damned one of them. He counted at least two dozen of the beasts huddled together inside the shallow cave, but the shadows were deep and he suspected even more hid within. Nocturnal by nature, the beryaks slept peacefully while he spent the day carefully setting the traps. He was careful to ensure proper distance between them, cover each with snow, and leave the telltale markers on the trees so he could find them again. Exhausted, he headed back to his shelter.

His father's admonitions rang in his ears as his dogs pulled the sled back down the mountain. There were rules to trapping out here, he'd say, ticking them off one by one on his leathery fingers. Never come out here with less than a dozen dogs, sharpen your axe every day, keep the fire burning all night, and never take more than two dozen pelts a trip.

The last had always seemed strange to Ffnard, but as often as he'd pressed his father on it, he'd never gotten a satisfactory answer.

Settling in that night, the dogs penned, he sat by the fire, drinking his Hoggian whisky and sharpening his axe. He'd always followed his father's rules, but this year... this year was different. The roof was leaking, and his wife wouldn't stop squalling about how the fences needed mending. Ffnard needed more money, and that meant more pelts – two dozen wouldn't cut it this year.

Eventually, he drifted off to sleep. The fire burned all night.

***

The next morning, the lair hadn't even come into sight yet when he first heard the howl of the trapped beast. Ffnard grinned. It was crying for help that wouldn't come – beryaks didn't know much, but they did know enough to leave their wounded behind. They would stay within their cave, knowing what safety they possessed came from numbers.

Pressing his dogs eagerly, he approached the trapped animal. It lay on its side, froth collecting at the corners of its mouth, eyes rolling wildly. Its right leg was caught in the trap, and Ffnard could see bloody red gouges in the white fur where it had tried to chew off its own leg. The beryak's chest heaved and the muscles in its neck tensed as though it were screaming, although only a raspy rattling emerged. He had seen this before – the shaggy bastards would scream for so long, they would tear their own vocal cords.

"That's what ye get fer bein' stupid." he muttered, driving his axe into the bony ridge between its eyes with deft precision. Its muscles tensed, then relaxed. Two dark eyes focused briefly, before clouding over.

The beast was dead, and Ffnard set about claiming his prize, the first of many that day.

***

By the second week, the beryaks seemed to recognize that something was different. Ffnard caught a group of them out late one evening, just before the sun had set. Shambling around the cave entrance, they were staring intently at the ground in front of them as they walked. He sat and watched them, gnawing absent-mindedly on a piece of jerky. They poked and prodded the earth, occasionally looking up and grunting.

Finally, he shrugged, climbed onto his sled and started back. It was dark by the time he returned to his encampment, and the wind whistled through the pines behind the shack. The snow crunched beneath his feet as he penned the dogs, and they whined and yipped as Ffnard tossed them their dinner. Turning back towards the shack, he had a sudden feeling of eyes upon him, cold and inhuman. He whirled around, his hand on his axe, expecting to see a beryak rearing up, claws flashing, but there was nothing.

No movement, no sound, only the glistening of the moon catching stray snowflakes as they drifted softly from above.

"Vorn's nails!" he laughed uneasily, his voice shaking only slightly.

Though his heart still beat wildly, he dismissed his momentary panic as the sorts of imaginings that come from too long with only dogs for company. Glancing behind him as he headed inside, he promised to pass on the whisky that night, and get good rest.

***

The next morning, the dogs were strangely quiet, and a foul odor lingered about the trees. It was a damp, fetid stench and while the dogs didn't struggle as he harnessed them, they weren't cooperative, either. They simply sat, stock-still, as though they could sense something, and he felt the tension in their muscles as he secured the straps and fastens around their bodies.

Had Ffnard looked back towards the shack as he and his dogs headed out that day, he might have seen two strangely shaped patches of ice, one on either side of the window that overlooked where he slept. Two patches of ice that resembled inhuman hands, placed where something might brace itself when looking through the window.

By noon, they were melted and gone.

***

That day, he caught four beryaks, a real milestone – it brought his total to thirty. He set the final pelt carefully on the sled, and then walked the area, methodically checking each trap. As he went, he passed the time by counting off his expenses in his head, calculating the number of pelts he'd need to sell to cover them. As the sun began to sink on the horizon, Ffnard was feeling good. This would be a good year. A profitable year.

He was securing his sled when he again felt that peculiar feeling, that sense of vulnerability and exposure. His breath froze in his chest and he stood, reaching out with his ears as his father had taught him. The snow had a way of muffling sound, but aside from the creaking of tree limbs and the wind skittering off of packed snow, he heard nothing. He swore he caught that odor again, but the cold deadened his sense of smell to the point where he couldn't be sure. One of the dogs growled, low in its chest, and crouching, Ffnard brought out his axe. He peered intently and there, at the edge of his vision between the trees, he caught a brief glimpse of... something. A flash of movement in the fading light, pale and hairless, there for an instant and then gone again just as quickly. He took a step in that direction, perhaps intending to give chase, but the bellow of a freshly woken beryak gave him pause. Chasing after phantoms in a forest full of beryaks was not how he wanted to spend his night. Whatever it was, it seemed frightened of him, or at least reluctant to get too close, and that was good enough for him.

Climbing onto his sled, he set the dogs back on the path, and headed to the shack.

Whatever it was, it didn't bother Ffnard the next day, or the day after that. He was grateful—he had no time to be concerned with such things, and he quickly put it out of his mind. While he occasionally wondered at what that something might have been, most of his time was spent thanking Vorn for the abundant supply of albino beryaks, and going about his business.

By the third week, though, Ffnard swore they were getting smarter. As he made his daily rounds, he began to find traps that had sprung, but gave no indication they had caught anything. It even appeared that there were traps missing altogether. Strangest of all, he found traps that appeared to have frozen solid, and then broken. Picking up the remains, he found them brittle, and they cracked and crumbled in his hands.

If that weren't bad enough, the lurker had returned, and it too had learned. It didn't get close enough for Ffnard to sense it anymore, but the scent was unmistakable, and each morning, he'd find the dogs huddled in their pen growling. Once, he was awoken by frantic barking from the pen. Racing out, axe in hand, he found nothing but whining dogs. Sniffing the air, he again caught the scent.

"I know yer out there!" he bellowed into the darkness.

Silence was the only reply.

Cursing, he took a long swig from the flask that had become his constant companion, and went inside. He didn't get much sleep that night.

***

The day had been much like those before it. He'd walked his trap line, collected his pelts, and kept a dog at his side in case the mysterious watcher came too close. His caution slowed him down, though, and it was late in the day by the time he was through. He secured the day's pelts to the sled, secured the dogs, and began down the trail to his encampment. Biting his lip, he found himself glancing nervously over his shoulder at the setting sun as they made their way. The peaks in front of him were already half cloaked in shadow, and daylight was fading fast. After the incident the night before, he'd wanted to have the dogs penned by the time the sun set, but it didn't look like he was going to make it.

Concerned as he was about the time, and the sun, and the dogs, Ffnard never saw what it was that startled the lead dog. They were rounding the corner on the path leading back to the bottom when the lead, typically a stolid, unshakeable type, suddenly jerked to the left and lost its footing. The dogs yelped as one in surprise, and the sled skewed sharply to the left and over the edge. Ffnard was thrown from the seat as the sled dropped from beneath him. He had the presence of mind to hold onto the leashes, but saw the ground far below and shut his eyes.

***

Time passed, he didn't know how long, but finally his eyes opened again. He saw a hole above him, and the weak light of the moon reaching tentatively towards him from far away. His lips moved, but they were cracked and dry. Licking them was pointless; his tongue had no moisture to share. Strangely, he felt no pain. He must have been lucky, indeed, to survive a crash from that height. Vorn was truly with him. Looking to his right, he saw the remains of his sled.

He heard the crunch of snow and a low whine in front of him. One of the dogs, he thought, and struggled to sit up. Pain flared like the fiery blast of a furnace, giving new life to dead nerves, and it consumed him completely. He fell back, and screamed.

As the pain slowly subsided, he forced himself to move again, starting with slight movements of his neck, then his shoulders, then his upper back, and finally he saw the damage, though he immediately wished he hadn't. His legs had broken like matchsticks against a rocky outcropping. He counted 3 compound fractures on his left leg and another on his right. Blood had dripped from the wounds and frozen into red icicles, hanging from his blue, exposed flesh, which was stuck to the rock like a child's tongue to the blade of a sword.

Frosttouched, he cursed. The cold had no doubt saved him, flash freezing his wounds before he could bleed out, but the flesh was dead, never to return, and surely he would never walk again. Of course even if he could walk, he had no idea where he was, or how to get to his encampment from here.

There was a wet snuffling from the darkness, and Ffnard reached to his shoulder for the axe, only to find it missing. Cursing, he reached wildly around him until his shaking hand closed over a rock, and waved it wildly in front of him.

"Hhhhh... hhhuh..." his voice cracked and he coughed weakly, "Hhhhhh...hhho there – stay back!" One of the dogs, a female, limped towards Ffnard, walking in a strange manner. The dog's leg had snapped almost entirely in two. The dog paid it no heed, however, and it walked on the stump of bone, leaning forward heavily to accommodate the shortened limb. Its paw dragged behind, held by a flap of skin and a bit of muscle. Looking up, he realized that one of the dog's eyes was cocked off at an upward angle, the white shot through with red bright enough to stand out, even in the dim light. Milky fluid flowed freely from its black nose, spilling to the icy floor. The dog had bitten its tongue, which now hung limp and blue from between cracked teeth.

He desperately pushed himself away from the advancing horror, detonating an explosion of pain when his shattered legs shifted and his frozen flesh tore free from the ice.

The dog reached down and firmly grabbed a hold of the furs that had once protected Ffnard and dragged him forward; that unblinking, bloodshot eye staring directly at him now as he slid out from the circle of light and into the darkness.

He attempted to swat the dog, calling it in a croaking voice, but it ignored him. His strength exhausted, Ffnard collapsed and accepted the inevitable. It was only once he was freed from the burden of sight that he realized that heard no sound of breathing save his own. There was no panting from the dog; it seemed to feel no exertion from the effort of dragging him. Was it dead? If it was, did that mean that he was dead as well?

He thought he saw movement out of the corners of his eyes, but when he looked he saw nothing. Was he imagining it, or was something else down here?

Desperate to fill the silent void and chase away the terror encroaching upon his mind, he began to babble half remembered prayers to Vorn, mixed with pleas to the dog to turn around and return him to the light. His leg banged against the wall of the narrowing passage, causing phantom fireworks to explode in his field of vision and driving all thought from his head. The last thing he was aware of before the pain overtook him was the familiar stench of the lurker.

***

Ffnard dreamed of the sun. He dreamed of the fat orange disc, burning complacently in the sky, far, far away. He basked in its warmth as he lay upon an open plain, feeling its heat surround him, enfold him, cradle him. He pushed himself into the warm earth beneath, feeling the soft heat soothe his aches, ease the pain in his joints, relax his tensed muscles. He smiled.

But he came to realize that the sun was aware of him, that its alien intelligence had perceived him and more, that it was mightily offended by his presence. A dark maw opened wide within its circumference, and it gave a great bellow. The air burned and the ground shook and its rage pierced him like a thousand flaming arrows, pinning him to the earth. He felt its questioning probes, poking and pushing and burning. Such was the weight of its glowing thoughts that he felt his skin burn, then blacken, and finally peel away from the attention, leaving his innards exposed to the blistering scrutiny. Slowly the heat pushed aside organs, wormed between bones and slid across muscle. He screamed, but something crowded its way into his mouth, burning away gum and tongue and tooth, and he was choking. He was choking and burning now and even his tears were sizzling away on his cheeks or was that his eyes, burst and boiling away?

***

Ffnard awoke with a start, a scream perched at the back of his throat, ready to leap outwards. Looking wildly around, he realized he was back in his cabin and forced himself into calm. The sun was nowhere to be found, save for the tepid wintery light seeping through the gaps in the walls.

My eyes! He thought, his hands flying to his face, but his eyeballs were intact. With growing horror, he forced himself to look down, to gaze upon the wreckage of his legs. With timid, ginger movements, he examined himself, checking his neck, shoulders, arms, chest, groin, and finally he could delay no longer. Full of trepidation, he pulled back the skins on his lap and revealed... the same gnarled musculature that had greeted him last morning, and every morning before. Running his hands over every inch of his body, he could find no wounds, no harm.

Releasing a breath he wasn't aware he'd been holding, he relaxed and looked about the room. All was as he remembered, and what was that? The bottle of whiskey lay discarded, not far from where his hand had fallen the night before. A bit of the amber liquid still rested easily along the inside of the tipped over bottle. A bit of the light caught the glass, and Ffnard grimaced at the sudden flash. Vorn's nails but that light was bright.

He sighed. So that was that. An alcohol induced stupor, with some terrible dreams to pay for it. Gathering himself, he rose only to stumble, as his left leg was still asleep. Cursing as he limped to the door, he only realized as he opened it that he hadn't been awoken by the dogs. Shivering in the frigid temperatures, he limped around the corner towards the copse of trees where he kept the dogs tethered and penned.

"A'right, ye lazy bastards," he growled, "Bad enough I'm sleepin' in, but drink's me 'scuse, what's yers?"

He heard only silence, so he yelled again, "Dogs? Where are ye, y'mutts?"

Finally he crested the low rise, and stopped so suddenly his leg almost buckled beneath him. The pen, constructed by his great grandfather, made of sturdy oak and valonwood, had collapsed, and the thick leather tethers which had held his dogs as long as he'd been coming here were snapped. All of his dogs were gone but one. Slack jawed; he stared at the tracks left by the dogs in their mad dash for freedom. They went in every which way; there would be no following them, for sure. He sniffed the air, and sure enough, the stench of the beast lingered. Had the lurker released his dogs?

The one remaining dog whined, and crept towards him, nose to the ground, looking up at him. She knew her pack mates had been bad, and she snuffled his hand in abject contrition. Absently, he ran his hand through her fur as he looked around, still trying to understand what had happened. Walking back towards the cabin, he stumbled as he walked around the back, briefly registering annoyance at the pins and needles in his leg, but apprehension swallowing it as he saw a good number of the tracks going the same way, towards the sled.

"Aw no, not th' pelts!" he groaned. His slow gait quickened and, still limping, he started to run as he saw what was left of his sled, shattered and ruined. There wasn't a solid plank of wood left, and the pelts lay strewn about, ruined to a one. They had been ripped to shreds by savage claws, larger than a beryak's, and the air was thick with the familiar musky odor.

No dog's done this, he thought darkly. The creepin' bastard finally grew some balls.

If he read the tracks right, though, the dogs had... helped?

"Damn damn damn damn Vorn DAMN IT!" he howled, stomping around the area, picking up and discarding the pelts. Four Vorn-damned weeks of trapping and all of it for Vorn-damned nothing!

Breathing heavily, he stalked back to the cabin. Taking stock of his rations, he cursed himself again for a drunken old fool, cursed the dogs for the flea bitten mutts they were, cursed the mountain, cursed the bottle of whiskey and the Hoggians who made it but more than anything he cursed the foul smelling creature. He had rations enough to last a few more days, but with one dog and no sled, he wouldn't get very far, and couldn't bring much down from the mountains even if he did. He had no choice – it was back to Vayniris with him.

He gathered all his belongings, thinking of the story he would tell when he went looking for a whole team of dogs at the market, thinking of what he would tell his wife, thinking of how his family would get by until the far-gate opened again next year.

Whistling for his dog, he stalked down the path back towards the far-gate. He'd have to hurry—it was a half-day's ride from the gate to the camp; on foot he'd be cutting it close. The dog came trotting from the house, a spring in its step. She gently took Ffnard's hand in her mouth and tugged towards the path, eager to be on her way. Pulling it out of her mouth with a snarl, he hoisted his pack and stomped off down the trail, muttering to himself.

The Beast slid out from between the trees, pale and eyeless, slick with the blood of dogs. Far beneath the earth, it had tasted of this man, and would taste of him again, but not before it experienced this... City. A bit of the Beast walked at the man's side, reconstituted as the man had been.

The Beast was wary of the light, but the man and his dog each carried a bit of it inside them, which it could follow wherever they went. They were of the Beast now.

THE MONK AND THE RIDDLE

ALASDAIR CUNNINGHAM

In the days before the great storm there was a humble monk called Nyssa who had become lost in the Vale of Shadows, which was no place to be, lost or found. He was fond of daydreaming, and paid scant attention to the world around him, or the path beneath his sandaled feet.

After taking countless wrong turns, he found himself at a dead end. Before him lay a particularly nasty bog, filled with deadly quicksand and horrid creatures that bit you, and sucked your blood. He was angry with himself for allowing his daydreaming to lead him into this predicament.

"No more day dreams for me!" he shouted out loud. "From now on I will stop staring at the clouds and keep my feet on the ground." Sadly, it was not the first time that Nyssa had pledged this, and between you and me, it would not be the last.

The sun was dipping below the horizon and the fading light turned the fetid swamp water the colour of burnished bronze. There was nothing for it, he decided, I must retrace my steps and find a safe place to camp for the night. His heart sank at the thought of wandering clumsily in the dark.

It was getting cold now; there were storm clouds above and the rumble of thunder in the distance. He had taken but a few steps when large, fat, rain drops began to fall making his heart sink even further.

"Cold, lost and wet, what more can befall me?" he moaned to himself. One does not ask these things in the dark, especially in the dark of the Vale of Shadows. There are many things that could go wrong on a stormy night like that, and Nyssa was about to discover some of them.

It was night now, and Nyssa could not see his hand before his face, much less the thin rain-sodden trail he was trying to follow. He unslung his pack and took out his lantern. He rooted around for his tinderbox but could not seem to find it.

"Oh where are you? I know you are here somewhere, why, I used you just this very day when I stopped to make a fire for lunch..." he said aloud. No sooner had he said it, when he realised he had left it on a tree stump, many, many, miles from here.

"Can I be of any assistance?" said a voice from the gloom.

Nyssa jumped upon hearing it and dropped his lantern.

"I see you have a lantern but no means to light it; let me help," continued the voice.

And, as if by magic, a cheery yellow flame appeared from the lantern giving substance to the speaker. Before him stood a wizened old woman, with a hunched back and long greying hair. She was toothless and her eyes milky with cataracts. "Thank you kind lady, I will be on my way now," stammered Nyssa, fearing the old crone was a witch who was planning to eat him. Such is the way of strange old ladies that you stumble across when you are alone, and lost in the dark.

"Don't be so hasty young monk. My abode, as humble as it may be to one such as you, is not far from here. If you follow me, I can provide you with shelter and sustenance for the night. It will do you no good to be out here on a night like this; you never know what could happen...," she said with a sly wink and a cavernous smile.

She picked up the lantern but instead of heading back up the trail towards what Nyssa took for relative safety, she led him deep into the swamp. "Are you sure about this?" he asked." I am almost positive I saw a cheery little cave not very far from here."

"Fear not, young monkling, my house is built on sticks, and sits above the mud. It will keep you warm and dry and safe from harm."

Nyssa offered up a prayer of safety to Lord Buddha and followed the elderly lady. His manners would not allow him to refuse her request, no matter how apprehensive he felt about it. He only hoped that Buddha would hear his prayer and spare him a horrible death.

The going was tough, and more than once Nyssa lost sight of the bobbing lantern. The mud sucked at his feet, and tiny buzzing insects sucked his blood. It took them what seemed an age to reach the old lady's house. But, true enough, there it was: rising out of the swamp like a heron with wooden legs, covered with straw and giant lily fronds and slimy moss that glowed a sickly yellow in the dark. A cacophony of frogs heralded their arrival.

He climbed a makeshift ladder and entered the rickety shelter. The hut had a wooden floor and a small fire place. There were bones, large and small, scattered all over the interior of the hut. The monk felt his blood go cold. He prayed that his own bones would not be joining them. The old lady cackled and mumbled to herself while she got the fire going. There was a black iron pot hanging from a hook over the fireplace. Once the fire was nice and hot she pulled the pot over the flames to warm it.

The smell of whatever was in the pot made Nyssa want to vomit. But, like his fears, he managed to suppress it. She opened the pot and gave it one last stir, before she ladled the stinking bubbling broth into two wooden bowls.

"Here," she said thrusting the bowl at him, "eat this. It is very tasty and will give you strength, for that is what all growing monks need, is it not?" Nyssa took the bowl with trembling hands and looked at its contents. There was skin and bones, matted hair, and even what looked like to be an eyeball floating in the bowl. He put the bowl down and said, "Thank you for the gift of food, but as a monk, I am forbidden to eat meat of any kind. Such is the way of my faith."

The old lady looked very angry at this. The stew did indeed contain meat – that of a child she had stolen from a village on the edge of the swamp. It also contained a sleeping draught she had slipped, unobserved, into Nyssa's portion. She would now have to find another way to trap him.

Nyssa felt slightly relieved at not having to sample the foul contents of his would-be supper. However, the witch was not done with him yet. She turned around and rummaged for a bottle she kept hidden next to the fire. She took down two goblets from a shelf, and filled them. Again she secreted a measure of sleeping draught into one of the goblets and gave it to the monk.

"What is this?" asked Nyssa politely.

"It is only the finest sake in the land, young monkling. Surely even you cannot say no to such a delicious and warming beverage on a cold and desperate night like tonight?" came her reply.

"Again dear lady, as a monk I am forbidden to take in any strong spirits or alcohol, even for medicinal purposes. Such is the way of my faith," said Nyssa. He was beginning to feel rather pleased with himself, having escaped two potentially deadly pitfalls. If he kept this up, he might just make it to morning he mused.

So the old lady put down the goblets and said, "Surely you cannot refuse me anymore this night? Are monks such as yourself allowed to play the riddle game?"

"Why, of course Madam, even we are bound by the rules of the ancient riddle pact; in fact I like to think that I excel at it!" said Nyssa, his confidence returning.

"Good, good, good," said the crone, for she had a particularly hard riddle that none of her victims had ever managed to solve. "Then I shall begin," said she. The monk nodded in accord.

"Before we begin, what are the stakes?" asked Nyssa. He knew what she was going to say, he just wanted to hear it loud.

"If you win, monk, I will not harm a hair on your pretty young head, and I will guide you to safety when the sun is once more upon the land. But if you lose..." she said rubbing her hands together gleefully and smiling that toothless smile. "But if you lose, your life is forfeit and I will eat you as I have eaten all the others!"

"Deal," he said, "but if I win, not only will you not harm me, and show me the way out of this cursed bog, but you must swear never to lead another human being to their doom, to be eaten at your leisure."

She considered this for a second then nodded her head in acceptance. She was very old, and there were not many riddles she had not heard before; she knew she could win. Besides, she intended to eat the monk whether he won or lost; for there is no honour to be found in old ladies who live in swamps, and feast on the flesh of strangers.

They spat into their palms and shook hands, sealing the deal. "I shall begin," said Nyssa, and he asked her his riddle. He thought it was an exceptionally good one, having being taught it by Master Ekusa himself:

"There are four brothers in this world who were all born together.
The first runs and never wearies.
 The second eats and is never sated.
The third drinks and is always thirsty.

The fourth sings a song that is never good..."

The hag sat rocking on her haunches, her bony knees cracking and popping with age. Nyssa felt disheartened when he saw a cruel smile forming on her wrinkled face. "Four brothers? I have eaten more than four brothers in my time, I have eaten whole families and entire villages and tonight I shall dine on suckling monk!" she said, cruelly, "because I know the answer."

"The answer young monk is this: water, fire, earth and wind!" she cackled, and clapped her hands in delight. "And now it is my turn," she said, licking her lips and salivating in anticipation of the meal that lay ahead.

"A cloud is my mother.

The wind is my father,

My son is the cool stream.

My daughter is the fruit of the land.

A rainbow is my bed,

The earth my final resting place,

And I am the torment of man.

What am I? "

Despite all her cleverness she had forgotten one fundamental thing: never riddle with a monk unless you have time. And by time, I mean lots of time...

And right now, Nyssa had all the time in the world. You see, a daydreaming monk, such as Nyssa, likes to visualise the riddle from all sides and in all dimensions, both the seen and the unseen. There is no simple answer for a monk, such as himself. He needs to weigh all the possible responses. And so Nyssa sat back and let the Ki flow through his body, freeing his mind's eye to float above in the ether and contemplate the potential answers to the riddle.

Hours passed. The old lady added more fuel to the fire as the dead of night crept slowly on its way to morning. The sun rose and climbed to its zenith, forcing the wizened one to finish her supply of water. The hag tried to leave the hut to get more, but such was the force of the Ki emanating from the young monk that she could not. Lord Buddha had indeed heard Nyssa's prayer and had given him supreme protection, after all. No harm could the wicked lady bring to him when he was in this state, nor could she escape. She would just have to wait Nyssa out. And wait him out she did, for some time at least.

Nyssa's heart beat began to slow as his breathing became shallower. He wandered the universe in search of an answer. And slowly the old lady got older and thinner, dark her arts may have been, but they could not stand up to the power of the riddling monk who was locked in the arms of Ki.

And then, one day, the old lady died right there on the floor on which she had killed so many hapless victims. Still Nyssa had not given his answer. The hut fell apart over the following years, and the swamp slowly drained becoming a beautiful pasture of wild honey suckle and weeping willow trees.

Suddenly, one day, nearly ten years on, he finally had his answer. He opened his eyes and said "Rain. The answer to your riddle is rain!"

Nyssa saw what had happened and knew at once that Lord Buddha had kept him safe from harm; he had not aged even a day while in the void of thought. Nyssa stood up slowly and gazed in amazement at what had become of the foul swamp. He gathered some fruit and berries from the bushes and hedgerows close by, and drank his fill from a nearby stream. And with a song in his heart and a prayer on his lips, he headed back to the trail he had left all those years before, this time paying careful attention to where he was going. He had done enough day dreaming he decided. Enough for this life time at least.

UNDISCOVERED

JARED PLUMBER

I am cold.

Too cold.

I have stopped shivering.

The stone beneath me no longer feels cool to my touch. It's as warm to the touch as my flesh. Or maybe it's the other way 'round.

Odd. Until this moment, I have never thought of stone as 'cold.' Never in my life. It is the foundation of the Forge of Life, stone. Makes no sense to call it cold, as the warmth of Erivrim's breath courses through it. The whole cavern is stone. All stone. Should be warm, blessed by Erivrim.

"Oh, Erivrim! Hear my prayer!"

Was that my voice? Truly? It sounded so weak, so mewling, so....

Hoarse.

Koff. Koff.

So hoarse. Almost as if it had been strained. From yelling perhaps?

Or screaming.

Ah, yes. Screaming. I seem to remember some screaming. Oh, yes. There was a lot of screaming. Much of it mine, in fact. Strange to forget. I'm having trouble remembering a lot of things. I don't normally forget.

Koff. Koff.

It hurts to cough. Hurts bad. I'd like to forget the pain.

And the smell. I'd like to forget the smell, too. What is that smell? Rotten eggs. Rotten meat. A warm and fleshy smell. I've smelled it before. Can't remember. Hard to think. Hard.

The stone beneath me is hard. Cold. Unfeeling. I've never thought so before, but in this moment it's surely true.

"Erivrim, please forgive me! It is cold and hard. Forgive me this blasphemy."

It should be warm, soft. It has always been so. Has Erivrim taken the heat from the stone? Has Erivrim truly forsaken me? In this hour, in my distress, has He left me to suffer alone? Am I thus punished? The stone should be warm and soft.

Warm and soft. Like Marbryn.

"Marbryn."

I remember touching Marbryn's backside for the first time, as if it were yesterday. Touching...it was a pinch, really. Earned a good, hard slap in return, that did. And it was worth it. A nice bit of flesh, Marbryn.

And strong? She wields a hammer as well as any in the clan. Her arms are hard. Hard when she wants them to be.

I suppose that means she is hard too. But she's soft where it matters. Quite soft, in fact. Hard and soft. I got a kiss from that pinch too. A peck. Wasn't much, but still, it was a kiss. The first of many.

I yearn to hold her. Just one last time.

Oh, Marbryn. Remember me. You'll be hurt, I'm sure, when you get the news. Although I don't know who's to tell her. I'm alone, after all. I was the last. The last of this herlig. All the others, dead. A score of us. Dead before me.

I am lost. Lost and alone.

Bowels. The smell is offal. Guts. Shileg. Why am I smelling shileg? Oh, sweet Tel, the pain, the hurt, the smell.

Smells. Fresh bread on the hearth. Roasted meat on the spit. Give me these smells. Marbryn's stews, rich with gravy. Marbryn's hair, the first time we held each other in the dark. She smelled of warm, freshly turned soil after a rainstorm. Soil mixed with strawberries. Her hair. Thick. Clean. Now all I smell is fear, sweat, shileg. Not strawberries. Not Marbryn. Oh, Marbryn, I never meant to hurt you. I never wanted to cause you pain. I would never hurt you.

"Erivrim! I bid thee, care for Marbryn! Watch over her. Comfort her!"

Hurt. It hurts. The pain is sharp, biting. Though not as much as before. If only I could remember what caused the hurt, the pain. It is difficult to hold myself up. It hurts. This stone, the floor, it slopes downward. It is warmer now, the stone. Or maybe I'm colder. Can't tell. It's warm, though. Warm and dry. Dry on this side. Wet and sticky on that side. Odd. The stone, it is grainy. Gritty. Sandy. No, not sand. Not from the feel. Granite? Granite maybe. I cannot see it clearly. My eyes refuse to focus.

Koff. Koff.

On this side, the rock is sticky. Tacky. And my hand is red. Blood red. Blood. I can see that.

"Blood. Blood? Tel, who's blood is this?"

Blood. Shed blood. I remember shedding blood. I remember the first time. Cutting. Killing. I smelled shileg then, too.

Orc. 'Twas an orc. He wasn't big, as orcs go. A youngling himself, I wouldn't doubt. A youngling like I was. Erivrim's beard, it was a long time ago. A lifetime.

Orcs. It was orcs. I remember now. It was orcs this time. An ambush. They knew we were coming. Somehow they knew. They came from everywhere. This room was a dead end. A small room. Forty feet across or so. Large enough for fighting. But small enough to die in. Small enough that the noise was unbearable. Noise from everywhere. Shouting.

Shouting. Screaming. Yelling. And most of it ours.

Blood. Dying. And most of it ours.

My boys fought. They fought hard, they did. I remember that much. They brought honor to the hold, to the clan, to our people. They fought hard.

And they died hard.

They died cutting, smashing, slashing, punching. They died swinging and scratching. They died as dwar.

But still they died. One after another, fallen and slain. Fell to those tel-cursed orcish blades. One and then another, on this side and then that side. Orcs cut them down and they fell. Died. Dragged away.

And then 'twas my turn. They cut me.

Makes sense now, all this blood. It isn't all mine. But a good deal of it is.

Koff. Koff.

It is granite for sure. There's quartz and a bit of feldspar between my fingers. After all these years, my father's words abide with me. Granite. That would account for the echoes, the noise. The way the voices bounced and rolled through the halls. An excellent stone for music, my father always said. For echoes, for carrying vibrations. Sounds. Yells. Thundering. The calls of the orcs. The screaming of the dwar. Screaming.

Koff. Koff.

I fell screaming. The first youngling I killed, he died screaming. It's a shame: at the end I'm no better than an orc runt. Would've liked to have died better. Braver. No good way to die, really. Braver, I mean. Braver. Not screaming. Not like an orc. Not like a runt.

It's not like I've not been cut before. I have. My body is covered with scars. Never been cut this deep. I can feel things tearing with every cough, every movement. Like glass shoved in my guts. Cutting, biting, slicing, ripping.

Koff. Koff. Koff.

More tearing. More blood. Blood all over my hands. I have a lot of blood on my hands. I've had a lot, over my life. Killed a lot, I have. Mostly orcs. Never killed another dwar, though. Proud to say that. Never struck another dwar in anger, either. No reason to. "Hearth, Hold, Nation, Dwar," as the saying goes. "All else follows." My father taught me that. That and stones. He loved stones. There was nothing more beautiful to him than my mother and finely-dressed stone. He loved the feel of stone, how it talked to him as he worked it. He loved the smell of stone dust. Loved it more than he loved his children. I learned that from him, how to love something more than family. I'm sorry about that now.

"I'm sorry, Marbryn. Erivrim, tell her I'm sorry."

My voice. It echoes still, though weaker. It is not a large cavern, but I cannot see the other side. It is too dark to see. Strange. Too dark.

But still there's the smell. Oh, the smell. Worse now. Stronger. Acrid. Biting. Yet sickly sweet. A bit like warm, sugared meat. And blood. Lots of blood.

Bloody hands. Takes a lot to clean it off. Especially once it dries. That first youngling was the worst. I was young. Rash. Prideful. Bathed in his blood up to my shoulders. Laughed while I did it. Laughed with my friends. Later, I scrubbed for hours it seemed. Hours. Hot water, cold water. Even ice. Nearly drowned from all the washing. And froze, too.

Colder now than then. I cannot feel my feet. Toes won't move.

Koff. Koff.

Pain. It hurts. But not my legs. Legs just won't move. Legs wouldn't move when the orcs came, either. I froze. I'm shamed by that. By my fear.

"Oh, Erivrim, do not hold my fear against me. Allow me entrance to Glormalk. Let me wander its silver halls! Oh, Erivrim, forgive my dishonor, my fear."

I froze. Watched the others cut down; they fell and died, but I did nothing. Dragged away and I did nothing. That has never happened before. Not even against the Ridwolf giants up north.

I remember that fight; against the giants. I stood toe-to-toe with the Chief of the Ridwolfs, Glor-bur the Berserk and gave as good as I got. His furs stank of shileg and smoke. But I never shivered a bit. Answered blow for blow. His club, my axe. Around me, giants and dwar fell, one for one, until Glor-bur fell to my axe, his legs cut out from under him, his throat slit at last, cut through to the bone, never to move again. Then the Ridwolf ran. When Glor-bur died, they scampered like goats into the hills. I wept for the fallen of our herlig that day.

Even the dragon was not this bad. A small one, to be sure, but a dragon. Keledrargleof Nightwind. How could I forget? 'Twas a terrible fight. Acid spraying everywhere. Stinging. Burning. And teeth, oh the teeth. The stench of carrion. The biting odor of fear covered us all. It took all we had in us to fell the beast. The memories of that fight have given me many sleepless nights, for years. But even that was not like this.

There were just so many of them. They came from everywhere, screaming their obscene calls. All around me, my warriors died. They all died, and I? I did naught.

I saved one, though. Azkral. He was one of the first to fall. Crawled to me, dragging his useless legs behind him. 'Twas an ugly sight. Azkral, my son. My beloved son. Young. Marbryn will never forgive me for bringing him here, for killing him.

"Marbryn, I'm so sorry."

He crawled to me. Took him a while. I had already been sliced open, fallen to the ground. I saw him crawl; through my tears I saw him. Azkral. My child. He was nearly dead when he reached me.

I saved him, though. I had one healing draught left. Strong one. Lots of power. I had it out, pressed to my lips before I saw him, before he reached me. I stopped when I saw the fire in his eyes.

His eyes, so like his mother's eyes.

"Ah, Marbryn. Your eyes. Our son has your eyes."

Had. Had your eyes.

I held out the draught to him. He grasped it, just as he grasped my finger that day, so long ago, after he was born. He grasped it and I placed it to his lips. The healing was amazing. He was on his feet in no time. He was alive. Alive again.

I tried to warn him. Tried to call out. Instead, I coughed.

Koff. Koff. Koff.

He was cut down from behind. Orc took his head nearly clean off. Azkral, my son. My baby son. Marbryn, may you never know that I let him die. Believe, instead, that we died valiantly, died together; believe your son's blood is on the orcs' hands alone and no guilt shared by your husband, his father, who failed him. Not the nightmare this was. His blood spattered my face.

I tried, Marbryn. I tried to call out to him, our son. I tried.

I failed.

I was weak. Weak then; weaker now, of course. The blood. All this blood. Slow; 'tis nearly stopped. Cold. Can barely move. My son's body is right there. Right there, and I cannot reach him.

I think he's still there; I cannot see him. Dragged off with the rest, maybe. I cannot see him, cannot hold him. Cannot comfort myself with one last look at my son's face. Instead, he lies alone on the cold, hard stones. I'm sure he's still there. Still there on the stones, just beyond my unfeeling feet. On the stone floor. I have to believe that.

At least he died on granite, and not on sandstone. Or grass. But he died. He died, uncomforted, alone. Azkral died, betrayed. Betrayed by me, by my weakness.

"Erivrim, grant him entry to Glormalk. May Azkral be there to welcome me, may he forgive my mortal weakness, my failure to warn him, my failure to save him. Forgive me my traitorous voice, my treasonous mortality."

All I could muster was a cough. The slightest of sounds. No warning for him. Just a sound, a whisper.

A sound.

A sound?

"Who's there? Is someone there?"

I heard something. Someone is there. Some thing is there. It was a sound, like a footfall.

No. Not a footfall. Something else. What? I seem to remember. Yes. A hammer. This was more like a hammer. Like a hammer upon iron. One simple ringing note. I heard it. I know I did. A hammer, ringing. But it can't be. There is no forge here. It must have been an orc. It was a footfall. Or a sword struck against the wall. It was a sound to taunt me, fill me with fear. Tel, it's too dark to see anything around me.

"Show yourself, fiend!"

My voice. Weak. A whisper is all. It is unlikely anyone can hear me. My throat is dry. Raw.

Koff. Koff. Koff.

So thirsty. A bottle near my hand. I feel it; I cannot see it. A bottle. The healing draught. Perhaps...? No. Empty. Only a faint smell of lavender. But nothing else. Not even a drop to wet my lips. Certainly not enough to heal my wound. It healed Azkral instead. For all the good it did.

Sob.

No water left in my body for tears, even. Can't believe I'm weeping. Trying to weep. Trying. No tears. Marbryn says that weeping at times, 'tis not dishonorable. Marbryn. Oh, Marbryn. I will wait for you at the Gates of Glormalk. I will prepare a place for us. Azkral and I, we will prepare a home. We will await you.

Sob. Koff. Koff. Koff. Koff. Koff.

Surely they heard that. Whoever they are. My cough, it echoes. Even that weak sound jumps from the granite walls.

Koff. Koff. Koff. Koff.

Aaaahhh.... Tearing. I am torn. More blood. Darker. Heavier. Pain. It hurts, though not like before.

"Oh, Azkral. Marbryn. Marbryn, my love. Erivrim. Oh, Erivrim. Forgive me my weakness."

That sound again. Not footsteps. A ringing. Metal on metal. Not sword on stone. Again! Like an anvil struck by a hammer. Anvil. I remember my naming day. I heard that sound. That sound. I can still hear it. The anvil, pounded. Pounded. Pounded. Over and over. All through the ceremony. My father was there, looking proud. My mother, crying. And the hammer. Pounding. Ringing. While the Prestr chanted, the hammer rang. While the hammer rang, I was named

First Son of the Iron Pass. While the anvil shouted out, I was named Adrak. Adrak Yurlydd. Adrak Maagersson.

"I am Adrak Maagersson!"

Koff. Koff

Again, it rings.

Is it here? Am I here? Or am I in a memory?

I hear it. Ringing out. Singing my name with the Prestr.

"I am Adrak!"

My voice. Now less than a breeze. There is nothing left.

It is cold. The stone, the air.... Freezing. Hard to breathe. The smell of flowers on the cold air. No, not flowers. Grain. Wheat, of all things. Not even shileg any more. Wheat. Wheat on the cold air.

A little pain.

Now, none. No glass, no cutting, no slicing. Just slick. Icy. Cold. My eyes...I cannot see Azkral now. I cannot see where his body lies.

Koff.

Air is thin. Hard to breathe. Hard. Hard like stone. Hard.

Koff.

"Oh, Erivrim! Hear my prayer!"

The sound again. Ringing. My voice, what is left, joins with the ring. Echoes. The caverns are empty. I am alone with the dead. Alone with my son.

"Azkral, my son. Please forgive me."

Again, that sound. Ringing. Louder. It seems close at hand. But I see nothing. My eyes are dim. I am alone.

Alone. Alone and cold. There: a shiver. I feel little else. No pain.

***

Gasp.

What was that? For a moment, I was not here. Was it sleep? Did I dream? No. I am here. Alone. Cold. A wisp of wheat-scent as I move, ever so slightly. I cannot move more than that. Cannot feel. But for a moment, I could feel, move, run. For a moment, I was warm. It was not sleep or a dream. Much as I would wish it. Wishing. Wishing for a second chance. A second chance to see Azkral. To hold Marbryn close. Second chances. But it is not to be.

Not a dream, nor sleep. Then it was the Shroud, I'm sure, the

Shroud of Rinarg come at last to cover my head. Yes. The Shroud. Rinarg. Rinarg comes. We have met before, Rinarg and I. We have been companions on the field. Not friends, no. Never friends. But he comes. I can feel him here. Dark and vile, but necessary. Dark. Not evil, but uncaring. Unworthy. Unworthy in Erivrim's sight. He is Unworthy, and for the unworthy he comes. The unworthy and the forsaken.

Alone.

That sound again. And light. A light. Like a candle.

No. An ember. It is an ember, such as those at a cooling forge. It is flickering.

Strange. I am warmer. I cannot feel the stone beneath me. I cannot feel the guts in my hand. But I am warmer. The air remains thin. Thin. Hard to breathe. Filled with the scent of grain. But my heart yet beats.

It beats. I can feel it, beating stronger. No, not stronger. Harder. Hard. And the light, it flickers with the heart's beat.

And the sound. The sound rings, chimes, beats, with every beat of my heart. Rings with the light, flickering, ringing together. Slower. Longer.

Rinarg, the Unworthy One, is here. I can feel him. Greasy. His icy hands on my head. I feel... I feel....

Stretched.

Stretched and tired. No air. Harder to breathe. Cannot smell the wheat. But the hammer rings. My heart yet beats. And the light, the light grows closer. Slows.

"Take me, Rinarg!"

Rinarg. He shrinks away now. Backs away from me. Backs away from the light.

"Curse you, Rinarg! Take me and be done with it. Take me to your cursed halls, the Hearth of the Unworthy Damned. Take me! Do not play with me; I am forsaken by Erivrim, but I am still Dwar. I am not your toy; I am Adrak!"

I struggle. A breath.

Rinarg is gone. He has departed, leaving me alone. Even the Unworthy One finds me unworthy.

I am warm. A bit of wind. Warm hands on my brow, on my shoulders. Arms embracing me. Light. There is light all around me. I can see light. Warmth.

"Erivrim?"

No voice now. I have no voice. None at all. No voice, no breath. But an embrace. I feel an embrace. Hands on my shoulders, arms around me. Lifting me. Lifting me?

"ADRAK."

I am not alone.

Trying to breathe. Cannot. Cannot answer. No breath, no voice, no air. The light is steady now. There is no more beating, no more ringing. The stone beneath me is gone. There is nothing but the light. I am alone. I am not alone.

"PEACE, ADRAK."

I am discovered. I am found. I see...

"Erivrim!"

I am warm. I see...

"Azkral? Is it you, Azkral?"

I am warm. Found.

I am home.

THE EYE OF HYTUUZSH

ALEX J. CHRISTY

Lucas Clay gripped the wooden rail and closed his eyes, willing back the nausea that threatened to spill vomit from his throat. He stood upon the fo'c'sle of the merchant vessel and focused on the sound of the snapping sails as the ship tacked against the current. His dark grey hair hung in sweaty strands across his eyelids and chunky flecks of vomit decorated his short, scraggly beard. The man held no great love for ships, and this journey up the Grel River had done little to change that opinion. Unfortunately he wasn't there by choice.

It had been a week since the thrice-cursed dog Emilio Sheklas, merchant prince of Camarrak, summoned Lucas to his palace and showed him the contents of a small, lacquered box. Lucas had lunged at him across the table, and only the combined strength of three eunuch slaves kept him from killing the grinning merchant then and there.

"Find me the Eye of Hytuuzsh," Emilio Sheklas had commanded, plum wine staining his lips and teeth a deep violet, "or I will add more pieces to my collection." A few hours later Lucas was aboard a Camarrakan vessel heading north towards the ruined city of Hatal Chuut, thoughts of blackest vengeance bubbling in his mind.

The grizzled thief was roused from his dark thoughts as a quiet presence approached him from behind. He opened his eyes and glanced over his shoulder. On the deck a few steps from him stood Xoloka, half naked in a zebra-skin skirt and little else, her black skin glistening in the afternoon sun and a copper scimitar hanging from her hip. She seemed perfectly at ease upon the swaying deck. "Captain Tor wishes to meet with you."

Lucas leaned over and dipped his hands into a bucket of water, splashing some of the tepid liquid onto his face. He wiped his mouth and beard with a rag, and nodded at her. "Take me to him."

She led him from the fo'c'sle towards a set of stairs that descended to the main deck below. The hull pitched steeply and Lucas steadied himself against a heavy, iron harpoon gun. A relic from the merchant ship's days as a whaling vessel, Lucas found the bulky contraption comforting for some reason; perhaps because like him it didn't quite belong here.

Xoloka strode smoothly down the flight of wooden stairs, Lucas a few shaky steps behind. The crewmen averted their gazes as she passed, their attention quickly directed elsewhere. They had reason to be nervous. During their first day at sea she killed six of them.

Unmolested, the pair ducked into a doorway and headed below deck to the captain's quarters. Lucas stepped forward and knocked.

"Enter," said a deep voice from within.

Captain Tor Sheklas was the bastard son of Emilio Sheklas, although one would never know from looking at the man. Tall and strapping, with piercing blue eyes, a great mane of reddish-gold hair and a thick yellow mustache, there was little of his father in those features, and less of his personality. Lucas even thought he might like the man.

Captain Tor sat at his desk, a plate of salted fish and boiled beets before him. He looked up from his meal and waved Lucas to a seat across from him.

Lucas sat down. "Hello captain."

"Ho Lucas." The big man poured the thief a glass of bitter ale. They toasted, the captain emptying his cup in one before refilling it from a nearby pitcher. Lucas took a small, polite sip and set the glass down.

Xoloka moved over to a cot and stretched out on it, her green eyes focusing on the captain with feline curiosity. The big man glanced briefly at her then back at Lucas. "We near our destination. Another day or two of travel, if the winds stay favorable."

Lucas nodded and stared out a portcullis window. "Xoloka and I will need a small boat when we arrive, and provisions for three days."

"That can be arranged."

Lucas produced a pipe from his coat pocket and packed it with fragrant tobacco. "Anything else?" He struck a match and put it to the dark, sticky pipe weed.

Tor rapped his knuckles against the wooden desk and stared at his unfinished meal. "Yes, I have information you may find interesting. My father does not intend to send you alone into the city. He has ordered one of his men to travel with you, posing as a porter."

"Pilus?"

"How did you know?"

"He spends more time bent over the ship's rail than I do. Odd for a sailor, don't you think?"

"I suppose so."

Xoloka blinked serenely at the captain. "We can keep him in line."

Captain Tor scratched at his beard and nodded at her quietly.

"What?" Lucas asked, sensing more from the big man.

"I am coming with you as well."

Lucas chuckled. "I do not doubt your bravery or your skill my good captain, but this work requires finesse. I'm afraid your value is upon this ship."

"There is something I should show you." Captain Tor turned to a wall safe and unlocked it. From inside he removed a small wooden box, and placed it on the table. Within were two items: a piece of folded cloth, and a leather pouch. Xoloka climbed from the cot and walked over for a better view.

"You should know that you aren't the first my father has sent to Hatal Chuut on this fool's errand. The last expedition had forty men. Only one made it back alive."

Lucas shifted his pipe to the other side of this mouth and exhaled a sheet of smoke.

The captain continued. "The man was half mad and mostly dead when we found him, huddled in a dinghy drifting downriver. I recognized him as one of the porters, an amiable fellow named Lyle. We tried to save him but his wounds were badly infected. The poor wretch raved feverishly about many strange and horrible things before he died. Afterward, as the apothecary prepared him for burial, I noticed a small scrap of canvas fall from his hand. I picked it up and examined it. It was a map that pointed the way to the Temple of Hytuuzsh."

Lucas puffed thoughtfully on his pipe. According to legends, the Lost Temple of Hytuuzsh was an unholy cathedral located within Hatal Chuut. A singularly evil place, rumors were that King Kolophax had carried out blood sacrifices there to appease an obscure, pagan god. It was said that the old king sought immortality, and in so doing damned both himself and his city.

The Temple of Hytuuzsh was also the last known resting place of the Eye of Hytuuzsh, a giant ruby of unimaginable worth, and the object of Lucas' quest.

"Go on," the thief said.

Tor removed the cloth from the wooden box and laid it out, placing small weights at each corner. Upon the canvas was a hasty map sketched out in basic geometric shapes.

Lucas gave it a once over and shook his head. "This could be anywhere in the city."

"True," the captain said, "If one did not know where to begin. Not everything the porter spoke of was madness, my friend."

Lucas gazed thoughtfully at the captain. "What's in this for you?"

Tor grinned beneath his thick moustache and removed the small leather pouch from inside the box.

"The Eye of Hytuuzsh is not the only treasure to be found in those forgotten vaults. It is said that the Temple overflows with enough gold and jewels to make the Southern Kings sweat with greed. And I believe these rumors."

"Why?" Xoloka asked.

"Because of what I found in the porter's pockets." The big man emptied the leather pouch onto the table. Rubies, emeralds, sapphires, and topazes, each the size of a robin's egg scattered across the map, catching the lantern light and throwing kaleidoscopic colors around the room. Lucas and Xoloka drew sharp breaths.

The captain leaned across the table, eyes twinkling.

"How would you like to be very rich, my friends?"

***

The rowboat was lowered into the still waters of the small, moonlit bay, sending ripples across its silvered surface. Two porters took their places at the oars, while a third unhooked the securing ropes from their bow rings and signaled the sailors above. Soon the boat was drifting away from the anchored galley, oars tapping a slow rhythm as it floated towards the river.

Once out of the inlet the porters kept to the river's edge, guiding the rowboat between the tangled roots of giant mangroves. This far from the channel the current was sluggish, and the boat made swift progress. Around their boat slimy, glistening things slithered through dark pools and watched them with half submerged eyes. Plaintive animal calls echoed from the midnight jungle, some distant, some frighteningly near.

The boat scraped up on a sandy beach and the seven passengers climbed out, sloshing ashore and pulling the boat onto the bank. Ahead the jungle thinned a bit, and beneath the starry sky loomed a massive, black shape: The walls of Hatal Chuut.

Tor made his way towards the stone structure, axe in one hand, map in the other. As they approached, the sheer size of the wall became apparent. Standing at least a hundred feet tall, it stretched off for a mile in both directions before being obscured by the dense jungle.

Tor stopped at the base of the wall to light a torch. Lucas squinted as it flared to life.

"A bad idea."

Tor scanned the dark branches above. "I'll take my chances."

By the light of the flickering torch Tor consulted the map, and then gestured north along the base of the wall. The party followed a narrow path over roots and around fallen stones, their torchlight casting wild shadows about them. After nearly an hour Lucas stopped and knelt before a fallen tree. He took out his knife and started scraping yellow lichen from the underside of the log, collecting the gummy substance in a small glass jar.

"What's that?" Xoloka asked.

"Illok Urr, an exceedingly rare variety of lichen. It is the key ingredient in a deadly poison. With this sample and a bit of time, I should be able to concoct an antidote or two."

Tor snorted. "An odd thing for a thief to know."

"Everyone needs a hobby." Lucas looked up at the captain and smiled. "Mine just happens to be poisonous fungi."

"Why do we need antidotes?" Pilus asked, shouldering his way in. He was a pale, red-haired man with watery eyes that searched the thief's face brazenly.

Lucas picked out a small piece of bark from the collected lichen.

"There may be natives living within these ruins. If so, chances are they know of the Illok Urr and its properties. Having an antidote may prove useful."

Xoloka leaned in close to Pilus' ear. "Poisoned darts," she purred.

The pale man slapped at a mosquito on his neck and glanced around nervously. Lucas tightened a metal cap on the jar of lichen and stood. "All done."

The party continued north to a great crack that split the wall, as if a giant axe blade had fallen upon it from above. The fissure started about forty feet above them, and continued up another sixty feet or so to the top of the wall. Huge chunks of mossy stone littered the ground around them.

Tor turned to the expedition. "This cleft leads through to the other side. We'll need to climb here."

The porters began unloading their packs, producing several coils of rope, along with pitons, stakes and other climbing implements. One of the porters offered Lucas a pair of shoe spikes.

"Unnecessary." The thief took one of the lengths of rope and without another word began to climb. Despite the thief's growing age, he scaled the wall with a fluid grace. His practiced fingers found small cracks and imperfections in the stone surface, and using his arms and legs in concert he pulled himself up the wall with surprising speed.

In less than a minute he had reached the crevice; a narrow, wedge-like corridor, green with moss. Where he stood it was only a foot or two across, but at its apex it widened to at least twenty. Above that opened the night sky. Lucas tied one end of the rope around a jutting stone, and lowered the other end to the party forty feet below.

They climbed the rope one at a time and pulled themselves into the narrow crevice. The last to reach the top was the captain's porter, a stocky man with thick eyebrows and rough, weathered features. Lucas grasped his forearm, and the porter nodded his thanks as he clambered up.

The man was almost up when, from behind, they heard a flapping sound like the beating of great wings. He looked over his shoulder just as something huge fluttered up behind him. There was a blur of pale flesh and leathery wings, and then the porter was gone. A gust of wind whipped at Lucas' cloak and rustled the leafy branches of the trees across from him.

In an instant Tor and Xoloka drew their weapons. Lucas pressed his back against the wall and listened.

A few moments later the sound of beating wings returned, this time from above. They all looked upward, squinting at the black sky. They heard a wet, tearing sound, and a moment later a deluge of blood rained down on them, a gruesome torrent that drenched their clothes and doused their torches. Lucas pressed himself flat beneath a shallow outcropping and managed to avoid the worst of it. The others were not so lucky.

With a wet, clanky thud the porter's blood-soaked backpack landed on the stones between them.

From somewhere in the distance echoed a haunting peal, like that of a hunting horn. The flapping thing above them moved away at its call, and the night was silent once more.

The party stood in quiet shock, blood running down their bodies and forming small pools at their feet. Tor cursed quietly and Xoloka wiped her face with the back of her hand, glaring upward into the night sky.

Lucas stepped out from the alcove, only a few droplets of blood on his cloak, and picked up the dead man's backpack. He tossed it to Pilus, who caught it against his chest with a whimper.

Without a further word the party continued on towards the ruined city.

***

After about fifty feet the fissure opened up, and before them stretched the crumbling skyline of Hatal Chuut. Sloping roofs, golden domes, and spiraling towers sprawled below them, glimmering in the dim moonlight. Even in decay, the ancient city was beautiful.

Twenty feet below was an ancient warehouse with a partially collapsed roof through which they could spy the building's inky black interior.

"We need to make for that hole," Lucas said. "Before the creature that killed what's-his-name returns."

"His name was Philip," one of the porters whispered.

Lucas nodded. "Yes, let's not end up like Philip. I'll go first, wait for my signal."

Lucas tied off a length of rope and descended to the tiled roof. He picked his way over to the hole, avoiding the spots that seemed most damaged, and tied off a second rope. Signaling to the others, he dropped down into the black abyss.

The rest of the party followed, and they were soon gathered together within the warehouse. Ferns and wild orchids covered the floor beneath the collapsed roof, and the sound of dripping water echoed in the darkness. Tor pointed at an open doorway to the east.

Lucas nodded. "Stick close to me."

The party slipped out the door and through the lonely ruins, their soft footsteps making the only sound. Lucas led them down a long, dark alley between crumbling buildings, pausing now and then to scan the night sky.

After a mile or so the buildings to their left opened up onto a vast park thick with trees, ferns and wild grass. Ancient statues stood sentinel in the moonlight, almost unrecognizable beneath layers of vine and kudzu. Tor consulted his map.

"Now we head north." The party nodded their agreement.

Lucas led them into the overgrown park and they emerged from the dense foliage above a huge, circular depression ringed with concentric tiers of weathered stone.

"An amphitheater," Pilus said, slapping at the flies that buzzed around his face.

They descended the crumbling tiers to the floor of the amphitheater where the soil was dry and the air was strangely absent of insects. As they proceeded further, an acrid stench assaulted their nostrils. They soon found its source.

The foliage opened up onto a dusty clearing. In the center was a yellow pond of noxious liquid, partly obscured by clinging vapors. Along the pond's fulvous banks grew clusters of huge succulents, with squat stalks and eight-foot conical leaves, yellow as the pond, and with margins of sharp, foot-long thorns. Slimy, unwholesome mucus oozed from their hollow trunks in wet, bubbling patches.

Lucas turned to the party. "Do I really need to warn any of you to stay away from those?"

Pilus and the others shook their heads and Lucas nodded at them.

"Where's our other porter?" Xoloka asked, and they looked around.

They spotted him then at the edge of the pond relieving himself next to one of the giant, funnel-shaped plants.

"No you fool!" Tor yelled.

The porter glanced over his shoulder. In a blink the nearest plant leaned down and scooped him up, enveloping his body like a giant seedpod. The top of the plant cinched, the thorns interlocking like teeth. Within the plant's hollow body the terrified porter twisted and thrashed, his face pressed against the translucent yellow walls and his hands beating madly.

Tor and Xoloka drew their weapons and rushed to his aid, but skidded to a halt as the other succulents began shuddering to life.

The porter's muffled yells quickly turned into gurgling screams as yellow liquid filled the semi-transparent chamber. The liquid rose rapidly around him, turning pink and then red before frothing and sputtering from the puckered opening at the top. The thrashing inside the plant slowed and stopped.

Heedless of the other carnivorous plants, Tor bellowed and leaped forward, bringing his axe down on the succulent holding the porter. Its yellow flesh split vertically, spilling a red, watery mess onto the parched dirt. Tor jumped back from the sizzling juices, the tips of his boots bubbling and smoking. As the last of the liquid emptied the remains of the porter tumbled out, his body little more than a pinkish skeleton.

Pilus vomited onto his chest.

"Let's just go," Lucas said.

The shaken party shuffled out of the clearing, leaving the porter's meaty skeleton behind. A hundred yards from the amphitheater they emerged from the park and found themselves standing before a long cobblestone boulevard that ascended a hill to the north. Elegant marble buildings lined either side of this promenade, their structures relatively intact compared to the ruins elsewhere in the city.

At the far end of this boulevard loomed a gothic temple, its central dome of fiery brass topped with a single black minaret that climbed into the night sky. Lucas walked up and stood next to Tor.

"Is that the Temple of Hytuuzsh?"

"No, that is another dark place."

The captain led them northwest instead, leaving the boulevard to travel down a small side street. At the end of the lane was a building that looked much like the others; a marble structure with an arched doorway and tiled roof.

"This is it," the captain said. He strode up the front steps and through the doorway. Lucas, Xoloka and Pilus followed close behind.

The remaining porter approached last, huffing beneath the weight of two heavy backpacks. He was ten feet from the doorway when a whistling sound split the air and something clattered off the wall of the temple. Everyone looked down.

Lying on the cobblestones was a small, black-feathered arrow.

"Inside quickly!" Lucas hissed.

The party scrambled into the temple as more arrows ricocheted off the walls around them. Xoloka motioned Tor to one of the stone pews and they started sliding it towards the doorway.

The porter hustled towards the entrance, both backpacks swinging and clanging together. One of them slid off his shoulder and fell to the ground, spilling its contents across the cobblestones. He dropped to his knees to collect the items.

"Leave them!" Lucas yelled.

The porter stood, and two arrows punched through his neck and shin. His face pinched in confusion as he turned toward Lucas, and three more arrows burst from his chest. The porter then fell face first, his backpack pinned neatly to his body.

Lucas cursed and ducked inside, just as Tor and Xoloka upended the pew and slid it in front of the doorway. Another barrage of arrows bounced and skipped against the stone barrier, and then it was silent.

***

Tor lit a fresh torch and looked around the shadowy temple. More pews lay broken and scattered about, along with peculiar statuary and ancient, tattered murals. A stone altar built to honor some forgotten god squatted at the far end of the temple, small footprints criss-crossing the dusty floor before it.

He strode to the center of the room, his torch held high.

"The entrance to the Temple of Hytuuzsh is here somewhere."

"You mean this isn't it?"

"No, the real Temple lies beneath the city."

They walked around the altar and saw a trapdoor with spiraling steps leading down into blackness.

"Oh," Tor said. "That was easier than I expected."

The party followed the twisting stairs downward for several stories, the air growing colder and damper with each revolution. Finally they arrived at an old, wooden door, warped in its frame. Lucas inspected it for traps.

Satisfied, he tried the handle and found that it opened with ease. The party stepped through and into a corridor of natural stone. Above them stalactites dripped water into shallow pools, and a strange, black fungus covered the walls.

Lucas squinted closely at the fungus and then looked over his shoulder.

"Don't eat," he stated flatly.

Xoloka wrinkled her nose at the unappetizing substance. "Give us a little credit."

The thief led them through the damp corridor. Gradually a pale, red glow began to emanate from up ahead. They extinguished their torches and edged towards the crimson light.

After a few hundred yards the corridor opened onto a vast, subterranean cavern. The party crouched behind a cluster of crumbling stalagmites and gazed in wonder at the macabre chamber before them.

An ossuary of sorts, though without any pretense of reverence or sanctity, the cavern walls danced with the ghoulish ivory of countless human skeletons. Embedded within the walls and ceiling, these bones had the appearance of having been forced through the stone from the other side, rather than carefully placed. Thousands of skeletons burst like this from the cavern walls and ceiling, their spines twisted in ancient agony, their jaws hanging open in silent screams.

"The Temple of Hytuuzsh," Tor whispered.

From the vaulted ceiling above hung hundreds of stalactites, each tapered shaft carved with intricately detailed motifs depicting pagan practices of the most vile nature. The nearest column detailed scenes of human sacrifice, cultists coupling with inhuman monstrosities, and twisted, tentacle-wreathed gods devouring worshippers like clusters of grapes. Each stalactite was illuminated from within by a dim, red light.

Interspersed with these stalactites were the polished stumps of former stalagmites, now cut low and level. And seated upon these stumps, like pupils awaiting instruction, were two-dozen impish creatures. The wan red glow from the stalactites revealed scaled skin and wide expressionless mouths, grotesque claws where hands should be and yellow soulless eyes. The creatures chattered quietly with one another in a strange tongue.

"The Alauari speak of such fiends," Xoloka said. "I always thought them merely children's stories."

Standing before the congregation was another of their kind, taller than the rest with a flaccid mane of blue flesh around its head. It wore robes sewn from a colorful patchwork of cloth and skins, adorned with feathers, precious stones and bits of bone. Upon its head was an elaborate miter of worked gold and red gems, while in its hand it carried a wooden staff topped with a human skull.

The priest stood in front of a sturdy altar of black stone with a golden hand protruding from its center. The palm of the hand was hollowed out, as if to hold a large, round object.

"The Eye of Hytuuzsh," Lucas said, looking around. "Where is it?"

"I do not know," Tor said. "And I see no sign of any other treasure." With a furrowed brow he consulted his map, as if the answer lay there. Lucas scanned the cavern with his keen eyes.

Behind the altar, twenty feet up on the cavern wall was a small, dark tunnel. Beneath this shadowy passageway at the base of the cavern wall was a curved ivory horn, banded with bronze.

Lucas motioned silently at the horn and the dark tunnel above it. Tor and Xoloka nodded and moved off towards the tunnel, hugging the left wall while Lucas followed the right. Pilus remained behind, huddled next to the brittle stalagmite cluster with what was left of their equipment.

Lucas sneaked past the worshipping creatures without being noticed, and was nearly to the tunnel when a loud crash rumbled from behind him. He looked back to see Pilus picking himself up from the floor, broken remnants of the stalagmites around him. The thief cursed under his breath.

At once the scaled creatures turned and hissed, jumping from their stone seats and drawing obsidian weapons. The priest's neck flange opened into a shuddering fan of bright blue skin as a loud trill emanated from its swelling throat. It pointed its skull-adorned staff at Pilus and waved it menacingly.

Lucas then appeared calmly behind the priest and slipped his dagger into its back. The creature's warbling cry cut short and it crumpled to the floor.

The fiends ceased their gesticulating and regarded their fallen leader with curious, tilted heads. Tor and Xoloka took the opportunity to charge from their hiding spots into the flank of the distracted creatures.

With a metallic ring Xoloka's scimitar was out. It flashed diagonally one way and then the other as she spun through the group of creatures. Two misshapen heads flew to her left, a clump of entrails and various limbs to her right.

Tor's charge was less graceful, though just as effective. Shouldering one creature out of the way, he blocked the thrusting spear of another with his axe. In the same motion, he brought his weapon up and shaved off the front of that creature's face. A third fiend sprang at him from his left. Tor grabbed it mid leap, lifted it up over his head and impaled it on a low hanging stalactite. He held it there, blood from the dying creature pouring down on him, his blue eyes gleaming with barbaric rage. The remaining creatures broke and fled down the corridor.

Tor pulled the creature's carcass from the stalactite and tossed it aside, walking with Xoloka to the altar where Lucas was cleaning his blade. Pilus shuffled up as well.

"Nicely done," the thief said.

From behind the altar a trumpet sounded, loud and hollow. One of the creatures crouched at the base of the wall beneath the dark tunnel, its thin lips blowing on the ivory horn. It glanced sideways at them and ran off.

Tor chased the small bipedal thing as it scrambled towards a portion of the cavern wall devoid of skeletal decor. There was a heavy click followed by a low, scraping noise and the wall slid open to reveal a hidden chamber glittering with piles of gold and gems. The creature ducked in, and the panel shut behind it.

Captain Tor skidded to a halt and pounded his fists against the stone wall. "Did you see that?" He slammed his fists into the wall again. Lucas and Pilus ran over to him.

Xoloka stared at the horn, a thoughtful expression on her face.

"Step back, captain," Lucas said. "Brute strength will get us no closer to that treasure." The thief ran his fingers along the wall, his ear pressed to the stone surface.

"That horn call sounded familiar, did it not?" Xoloka asked.

Pilus shushed her and pressed his ear against the wall as well.

Lucas stood abruptly, his expression crooked. "She's right."

A heavy, flapping sound echoed from behind them near the altar. Lucas and the others looked over their shoulders.

Upon the lip of the tunnel above the altar squatted an abomination; a nightmarish, winged thing partly obscured by the shadows of its dark lair. Great leathery appendages sprouted from its torso, fluttering in the small space. Its spindly claws gripped the remains of Philip, now little more than a ragged clump of meat and clothes.

What was worse, the creature's face was shriveled like that of an old man, with two lifeless black pits in place of eyes and white hair falling around its bony shoulders. It leaned down and casually tore a moist chunk from Philip before lifting its head and watching the party, its mouth working noiselessly, its chin soaked in red.

"King Kolophax," Lucas whispered, numb with horror.

From the center of the thing's back writhed a grey, fleshy tentacle that gripped a ruby the size of an ostrich egg.

Captain Tor pointed to the waving appendage.

"The Eye of Hytuuzsh!"

Xoloka adjusted her scimitar in her sweaty palm. "You do see what it is attached to, yes?"

"Bah!"

Dozens of chirping cries echoed from the corridor behind them, along with the sound of claws scraping on stone.

"Not good," Lucas said.

"Hold them off while I get the stone." Tor stepped forward.

The monstrosity that was Kolophax let out a horrible moan from its blood-drenched mouth and tossed Philip's corpse to the side. Its wizened face stared at the captain for a few moments then it defecated loudly on the stones and climbed down to the cavern floor, where its wings unfurled to their full extent. The Eye of Hytuuzsh wavered at the end of its long tentacle and then focused on the stalwart captain. The gem began to glow with a bright, crimson light.

Tor squared his shoulders and hefted his axe.

There was a faint, ultrasonic ringing and a beam of red fire erupted from the glowing gem, bursting towards the captain like a molten spear. Tor rolled to the right, avoiding the beam. The Eye released another beam and he raised his axe to deflect it. The crimson ray bounced off the polished steel surface of his axe, angling wide and hitting Pilus square in the face. The man's head burst into flames and he stumbled a few steps before falling to the ground.

Again Kolophax attacked Tor, swiping with claws and hooked wings. Tor dodged to one side then lunged forward with a swing of his axe, shearing off a ribbon of flesh from the creature's meaty thigh. The monstrosity howled in anger, white pinpoints of light flaring in its black eye-pits. It unleashed another molten lance of fire at the wild captain. Tor sidestepped to the left as the ray caught the trailing end of his cloak, setting it ablaze. He tore it off and hurled it aside.

Behind the party a group of scaled creatures emerged from the corridor. They drew small bows and nocked black-feathered arrows into them. Lucas and Xoloka took cover behind the altar as these fiendish archers released a fusillade of arrows. The projectiles whistled around them, bouncing off the cavern walls.

"Get to the ship you two," Tor said, a small arrow protruding from his calf. "I'll meet you there." He slashed at Kolophax's wrinkled, hissing face, holding it at bay.

"I can't leave without the stone," Lucas said.

"Run," Tor yelled. "Now!"

Xoloka pulled Lucas towards the back wall where they climbed the uneven surface and scrambled into the dark, nightmarish tunnel. The pair crawled through piles of wet, reeking guano and past the mangled body of Philip. The carcasses of older meals littered the tunnel as well, reeking of rot and crawling with maggots. Lucas covered his mouth and glanced back, catching a quick glimpse of Tor wrestling with Kolophax, his hands around the thing's thrashing tentacle as they tumbled out of sight.

After forty feet Lucas and Xoloka emerged from the tunnel into the humid, night air. They found themselves on a small ledge jutting from the face of a sheer cliff, the Grel River churning sixty feet below. The pair paused uncertainly before the dizzying precipice. Then an arrow buzzed between them and without further hesitation they leaped from the cliff.

**

Two crewmen hauled the drenched pair from the small rowboat and onto the deck of the ship, where they collapsed.

The first mate rushed over and knelt down next to them. "Where is Captain Tor?"

After a brief explanation of what transpired in Hatal Chuut, the first mate nodded grimly and ordered the crew to draw anchor. The galley was soon out on the river, traveling swiftly southward.

Lucas leaned against the mainmast, staring out over the water. Xoloka stood next to him.

"What will you do now?" she asked.

Lucas smiled at her, his face pale and his eyes darkly circled. "I'll think of something."

Just then there was a loud, wet thud from their right as a body slammed down onto the deck; mangled, burnt and peppered with arrows. It was Captain Tor.

The big man stared upward into the night sky, bellowing in laughter. In one meaty paw he grasped a limp, grey tentacle, from the end of which dangled the Eye of Hytuuzsh. Lucas and Xoloka rushed to his side.

"I told you I'd be back," Tor said, grinning at them through bloodstained teeth.

"Aye, that you did friend."

Tor looked over their shoulders and clenched his jaw. "Beware, old King Kolophax comes for what's his." And with that the captain closed his eyes.

There was a cry from the crow's nest then as the winged abomination flapped into sight above the ship's billowing sails. Black ichor streamed from its body in a dozen places and one of its wings twitched awkwardly. The tentacle stump on its back whipped and thrashed wildly, spraying inky blood across the white canvas of the sails. It seemed that Tor left it in equally bad shape.

But even with such injuries Kolophax deftly snatched the lookout from the crow's nest and flicked him screaming into the river. The crew shouted and scrambled to defend themselves.

Lucas and Xoloka dragged Captain Tor beneath a wooden awning as crewmen raced frantically around them. Once safe, Lucas slipped up the stairs towards the fo'c'sle, a determined glint in his eyes.

Kolophax wheeled and came in low at the galley, slashing at the helpless crew with its wicked claws. Two men were dismembered where they stood, and another three were driven over the rail into the river.

Kolophax flapped around for a third pass when a sharp thrum emanated from the fo'c'sle, followed by a harpoon streaking silvery-blue through the night sky trailing a rippling line of rope. A second later the barbed spear punched through Kolophax's bloated abdomen with a wet popping sound and the abomination jerked backward, shrieking and thrashing as the jagged weapon tore at its stomach.

Lucas stood rigid at the heavy iron harpoon gun, his pale face a mask of murderous vengeance. He grabbed the crank with both hands and began to reel the creature slowly in. Fighting against the tug of the harpoon Kolophax flew low, flapping desperately just above the river, its old man face howling in pain as its wings slapped the water's surface.

Then without warning a colossal, scaled head erupted from the water, snatching the winged thing in its massive jaws. The giant crocodile bit down, and Kolophax burst in an overflowing mouthful of black entrails and body fluids.

With a great wave of displaced water the crocodile sank back into the river, pulling the rope tight and causing the galley to list to port. Lucas grasped the harpoon gun as the deck began to tilt.

From his left Xoloka vaulted gracefully over the main deck railing, her expression focused and her scimitar out. In one fluid motion she landed and cut the rope, and the boat rocked back to an even keel.

The pair watched quietly as the crocodile's thrashing tail disappeared beneath the dark waters.

***

Lucas Clay sat in front of his desk, a cup of tea to his left and a map before him. His hair was combed neatly behind his ears and his face was clean-shaven. A thin, ivory pipe rested in a cradle to his right, emitting a column of sweet smelling smoke. He reached for it and took a contemplative puff as his eyes scanned the map before him.

A moment later the door to his room opened and Xoloka stepped in, nude save for a bejeweled lion's mane draped around her hips.

"I have interesting news," she said, walking towards his desk.

"Oh?" Lucas took a small measurement from the map and made a note in the margin.

"Emilio Sheklas is dead."

"Is that so?" He blew on the ink lightly to speed its drying.

"He was being carried in his palanquin through Cathedral Square this morning when several worshippers heard a cry of pain from within. The merchant prince tumbled from his cabin moments later, hands and chin stained violet with spilt wine. He staggered towards a fountain and waded into its waters, whereupon he lifted his robes and forcefully expelled his entrails into the shallow pool. Witnesses say it was quite horrific."

"I imagine it would be."

Xoloka eyed him. "Was this your doing?"

Lucas pursed his lips and set down his pen. "I'm afraid I wasn't completely honest when I described the properties of the Illok Urr lichen that I found beneath that log in Hatal Chuut. For starters, Illok Urr is a contact poison. A single touch is all it takes to expose oneself. On its own the poison is quite harmless, however if it comes in contact with certain tannins it activates quite rapidly."

"What are tannins?"

"A variety of enzyme found in fermented fruits."

"Wine?"

Lucas smirked. "Wine is fairly brimming with the stuff."

Xoloka laughed and sat upon the edge of his desk, one long leg draped over the other. "Devil! So how did you deliver this poison to Emilio?"

"If you must know all my tricks, I coated the Eye of Hytuuzsh with the substance. I knew Emilio couldn't resist holding the gem in his own hands. And what would such an occasion be without a celebratory drink?" Lucas took a slow sip of tea and smiled. "All that was needed then was a careless toast or a flamboyant gesture; a single splash of wine to land upon his hand and mingle with the Illok Urr there. Frankly I expected it to happen sooner."

Xoloka swung her feet playfully. "So where does this leave us?"

Lucas motioned to the map he was studying. She hopped off the desk and looked over his shoulder. The map detailed the layout of a vast mansion or castle; a great gathering of rooms and hallways, each marked with tiny notations in careful penmanship.

"What is this?" she asked.

"It is a map of Emilio's palace." Lucas placed his finger on a small, octagonal room near its center. "Do you know what this is?"

She shook her head.

"Emilio's vault," he said. "Do you know what we will find in Emilio's vault?"

Her face lit up. "The Eye?"

"How would you like to be very rich, my dear?"

Xoloka's lips parted in a delighted smile and her emerald eyes glimmered with mischief. She looked the thief up and down, her face growing flush with an unexpected heat. Lucas opened his mouth to say something else, and without warning her lips were on his. He grunted in surprise as the weight of her body carried them both to the floor.

Whatever it was he had to say, it wasn't that important.

THE SUN IS WITH US

JOSHUA GRABOFF

The messenger found them in the mountains. He was drowning in his own sweat. He bled from half a hundred small wounds. "Prince Emmon is dead," he said between gasping breaths. Aurum bel Jennikar sank to his knees to lead his men in prayer.

That night, Prince Jennikar sat by his war table. The wind moaned through the rocky passes. His silken red tent trembled. Emmon Brightmane had been one of the keenest minds amongst the Sworn and first to battle. The loss of Brightmane and his clansmen would tell heavily on the war. Jennikar frowned and ran his fingers through his hair.

Brightmane, he knew, had hired up the Companions hoping to use them against the Ajathi. Jennikar's own contingent could catch up to the retreating force just as they reached the old fortress at the desert's very border. The Companions had to walk; no horses would bear their dread weight. Besides which, Brightmane had many men on foot in the border armies and Jennikar had only his mounted Sworn.

"Arah ijh irrikah," he muttered. The Sun is with us.

***

How long ago, Shade wondered, had they stopped using his name? He didn't even think of himself as that man anymore, he realized suddenly. The name had been shed, and so had the person. They had gone together, hand in hand into the grave. An apt metaphor, he cackled madly to himself. Like all of the Companions, he too had begun to loosen his grip around what it meant to be sane.

Every day he had to remind himself how to act lest he fall into a listless unsleep, a meditation in which the world mattered little.

He did the addition in his head, relying on the twitching of his fingerbones to remind him. Fifteen years, he thought to himself and then, no, that can't be right. He did the addition again. Twelve years, this time. That seemed closer to the truth. Though the truth was a shifting marker these days. It was as if he hunted for a minaret that had become buried by the sand. Every stone was a marker, every protrusion was the herald of the buried tower. He remembered that he had liked to wear rings. His fingers were too gaunt for rings now. They had been stripped of their flesh, the excess mercilessly scrubbed away by time and circumstance.

He rasped his fingers against the pale white curvature of his skull. Blackrot, ever easy to anger, spat at him to stay quiet and stop. Shade rolled his eyes, but obeyed. Everyone listened to Rot, because Rot was older and meaner and more cunning than the other Companions. He could be marvelously short-sighted too, Shade thought sourly. The Sunsworn for whom they had lately whored their steel had no love of the Companions. Shade knew this, Stump knew this, and he supposed Black must also know it.

Shade unfurled himself like a flag from the shadows in the dusty courtyard and went to go find someone other than Black or Fear to talk to. Black was always angry at having his thoughts disturbed and Fear was too inscrutable to even bother with. She always seemed as though she was smiling a cruel smile at you behind her grotesque eyes.

He climbed up to the walls where Hobble stood guard. The old sentry still had flesh on his bones, and it hadn't begun to wither and dry like that of the others, either. He stood with his curved horn bow strung and clutched between nerveless fingers. Shade clattered up to him from behind. "See anything?" he asked in a voice that was little more than a rasp.

The desert was a ballad of movement, all of it heat. The vast sea of dunes shifted drunkenly and lurched beneath the curtains of strange warped glass rising from their surface. Hobble shook his head. "Not an Ajath for miles and miles," he said. Shade peered out over at the spine of rocks that jutted out from the fortress like a long finger bone. "None that way either," said Hobble. "Trust me, I've looked."

"Why do we continue to fight for these Sunsworn?" Shade asked. His tone was quiet, the light of his eyes dimmed. His phalanges drummed against his ribs.

"What do you mean?" A great gust of steaming desert air blew through their clothes. They wore long robes, like the natives, though they weren't likely to overheat.

"They hate us," Shade said. "So why do Black and the others agree to work for them?"

"They hold our Contract," said Hobble simply. It was the holy writ of the Companions. The Contract, an ancient scroll venerated since they had first begun this task, passed down from one commander to another as the years or happenstance claimed them. Black was only the latest in line to hold the Contract and its list of names. The great list, the list that recounted every employer the Companions had ever served. Without the Contract they were nothing.

"I know that," Shade argued, "But why would they ever sign it in the first place? And why would Black accept?"

Hob shrugged. It was a mystery. Most of what Blackrot did was a mystery. He seemed driven by some endless anger. Many Companions were angry when they first arrived to serve, but Black had never let go of that hatred the others first felt on waking. He was like a living knot of furious muscle, corded up and incapable of releasing. A cramp upon the surface of the world, Silk had once called him.

Shade gave a grunt in return. "Who will be the captain when Black is gone?"

Hob blinked slowly. "Fear, I guess. Or Silk. Why?" Shade shook his skull. "I don't know if we can outlast the Ajathi and the Sworn," he said.

***

Mirth watched Silk watching the Sworn. He hated Silk for a myriad of reasons. He hated almost every one of the Companions, but he hated Silk most of all. The ancient creature was older than he was, and that contributed to it. Silk was the eldest of all the Companions and he acted it. Black raged, Fear smirked, but Silk studied. Of the three, he was the most infuriating. Truly, thought Mirth, it will be a pleasure when he is dead.

Now the eldest Companion had brought them into the Sworn temple to witness the nonsensical rights the Cultists of the Sun practiced. Silk was a believer in understanding the religions of all those that held the Contract—and those against whom the Companions made war, which were sometimes one and the same.

This particular ceremony was made all the more galling by its absurdity. Incense floated throughout the room, obscuring the vision of the Sworn (but hardly the Companions) and thus blotting out the very sun these Sworn purported to worship. A fat priest with a tremulous lower lip led the small cultic congregation in murmured prayer. Mirth thought he understood something about shadows and devotion, but he dismissed it as he shot another baleful glance at Silk.

He was, as his name suggested, wrapped in ornate bands of red and golden silk just for this occasion. Mirth sneered at him. He wore the same colors as the Sunsworn against Black's orders. Every Companion was supposed to wear black, the better to strike the hearts of their enemies. That was one of Rot's few changes that Mirth actually approved. It galled him to no end to see the masked Silk wearing colors out-of-regiment.

The fat priest intoned a low hymn, denouncing smoke and shadow and praising the sun. Any moment now, Mirth felt certain, and they would start slaughtering goats like their cousins the Ajathi. They were so similar that it pained him. What did they stand to gain by fighting one another? He sneered at them too. War was a fool's work. What was really vital was murder—feeling a man's lifeblood seep onto the ground. That was what mattered. He grinned at the thought. If he hadn't become moribund like the rest of the Companions, he was certain he would have risen in tumescence. Unlife changed things, gave one strange desires, and then took away the means to fulfill them.

There was a blare of trumpets from somewhere without. The fat priest's face split in joy. Mirth thought he looked like a squealing pig. Silk breathed in that whispery voice of his, "That signals the arrival of Prince Aurum bel Jennikar."

Mirth snorted. "Another prince? To replace the one we lost last week, is that it?"

Silk nodded. "It is said he is quite zealous."

***

Aurum bel Jennikar could not have been more zealous. He was raised in a Sunsworn monastery from the age of five and inducted into the cult proper as a priest at fifteen. At twenty-six, he was a towering figure within the Sunsworn temple. It struck him as a particularly bad omen that the rising sun heralded the coming of the Ajathi.

He despised the presence of the Companions. They could each feel his disgust radiating off of his perfumed body like sorcery. He was on the walls with them when the sun rose. He too saw the Ajathi lances and spears glittering against the lurid red eye of the dawn. The Ajathi rode out of the dawn, from the east, coming like vengeance. Many men whispered that it was blasphemy, a final proof that the Sun-god meant to abandon them to the Ajathi spears. Aurum bel Jennikar told them that it was a test. "The Sun-god means to measure our devotion!" he shouted. "Measure it he shall!"

As the prince led the Sworn beneath the cream-colored walls of the fort and into the field, he felt a strange sensation wash over him. The cool passage between the inner bailey and the desert was like the mouth of the great serpent of time that swallowed the Sun; the years were stripped away from him.

He remembered that the sweet salt-spray of the sea reached him even high atop the cliffs. He had come from the courts in the south where the horn of the land met the sea as it turned to encompass the world. There, at Ehndar, at the end of the world, there were no silver lamps or silken tunics. There were no musicians or storytellers. There was only the burn of labor. None of the monks so much as called him "my lord." The lowliest of the order addressed him just as though he were one of the servile.

But the Sun battered down on him as he emerged onto the field and the coolness of the tunnel shrank from his flesh. The past retreated to its proper place. He was no humble boy; he was Prince Jennikar who had weathered the scourging fire of devotion to come through clean of the little doubts that plagued other men. And yet, and yet; there were still things that assailed his bastion of spirit, such as the presence of the Companions amongst so many faithful, abominable in the eyes of Arah.

The Sworn assembled before their fortress, against Black's

recommendation. The Companions had wanted to hold the defensive, wait for the Ajathi to try to encircle them. Prince Aurum refused to hear of it. He spat, "We will do what the Sun-god asks of us and confront our foe like men, on the field of battle. Who holds your Contract, abomination?" he had asked with a horrible triumphant grin. He guessed at the sacred nature of the document and his suspicions were confirmed when Black had simply growled at him and told him to do whatever he wished.

Their beleaguered ranks were arrayed before the foe. The Sworn had been beaten back time and time again. The desert was their enemy as much as the Ajathi were, stealing their strength. Sworn were used to the rocky headlands of the coast, not these deep desert marches. Their mail overheated quickly in the sun; their own god betraying them. Shade had been the first to suggest to the Companions that they don the loose fitting robes of the Ajathi. It was Black who had demanded they be the hottest damn color on earth. While the Companions for the most part couldn't sweat, they could certainly feel discomfort.

They felt it now, at the center of the Sworn lines. They were stationed near the prince, at the fore, which Mirth felt was odd. He wondered at the cleric keeping them as close as he did; with the religious fervor that he felt, it would make sense to keep the hated abominations far away from his sacred person. Mirth touched his knives with anticipation. Yes! he exulted. It is coming! The contest, the battle of will where the sharper, faster, more brutal would win. His blood sang.

Aurum watched the Ajathi on the horizon. There were so many of them, all in drab brown colors with their armor hidden by their long robes. The sun behind them made it hard to see. He frowned at the horizon, his sword drawn, his horse stamping under him. The thousands of Sworn foot braced for the charge. There was a terrible calm, a murderous silence. Hands twitched in anticipation. Someone somewhere let off a nervous yelp. Mirth could hear himself giggling under his breath, like a run-away teapot boiling into the fire.

Then the Ajathi screamed a war cry. Distant drums and bells began to ring from somewhere behind their line. As one they lowered their lances. As one they charged. Prince Jennikar spurred his horse forward and shouted "Arah ijh irrikah!" he screamed. The Sun is with us! The cry went up from amongst the other Sworn. The Sun is with us! But the Companions did not whoop, or cheer, or holler. They went to their task like grim workmen. Black raised the standard, a deep night-blue field with a clenched skeletal hand upon it. The whole Sworn army began to canter forward.

Ajathi screamed down the sloped sand, their riders hollering in booming chorus. Fear began to chant; burning words erupted from her flesh, lances of fire shot toward the advancing enemy. The rest of the Companions joined in the charge of Sworn swords and whirling maces. Censers, held by the cult-priests in the rear, kicked incense up into the field making everything smell of cloves. Fear's fire turned aside; the Ajathi must have sorcerers hidden in their ranks, dressed as warriors or princes. The lances curved up into the sky, deflected by invisible wardings.

Then the lines came together. Ajathi shields splintered beneath the heavy Sworn lances and two-handed scimitars. Their scaled armor cracked and broke. Bones shattered. There were screams. A few marks of sorcerous light identified those who were more than just lancers; the Sworn facing the sorcerers were thrown back by concussive booms and rolling thunder. But they were not enough. There were perhaps three sorcerers, maybe four, and they could not stem the tide. The Sworn were winning. Slippery in blood, Black cleaved his way through the desert raiders. His northerner's blade, straight but brutal, crushed as much as it cut, sending men plummeting to their death from horseback to be kicked to bloody paste beneath the hooves of their allies.

And then the Ajathi lines disintegrated. Jennikar seemed to be the only one who realized what was happening. A ruse, it was a ruse. They had abandoned the choice position of fighting with the sun at their backs to trap the Sworn army; on either side of the Sworn position, thousands more glittering Ajathi lances could be seen. Behind them, the numberless desert soldiers who walked on foot, bearing massive horn clubs or simple cutting tulwars, beat their drums and their gongs. "Arah abandons us," he said softly, his finery soaked in the viscera of fallen men.

Mirth alone saw Prince Jennikar look at Black. He alone saw the priest-prince make the decision. "Abominations," Jennikar said softly. "It is because we truck with abominations." Somewhere nearby, the

Ajathi were crushing into the Sworn flanks. Sworn men in red found their garments soaked a deeper hue. The bodies of footmen were flung aside by the charge of the Ajathi horse. Jennikar looked over at Black who was struggling with a knot of Ajath riders who had broken ranks and swept into the Sworn heart.

His sword rose. His sword fell. Mirth felt the longing of battle in his groin and said to the prince in a deadly flat tone, "I don't care what side you fight for, you will be my first." Mirth cared little for the sacred Contract. As Black fell, Mirth launched himself up at the prince, his blades drawn. The prince, the captain, and Mirth all went down amidst a tangle of blades.

The work was bloody, and three times the Sworn seemed ready to break. When Jennikar vanished beneath the press, many of the priests fled to the gates of the fortress where Ajathi outriders cut them down. But the first time, Silk stood high atop the piled dead and rallied the wavering Sunsworn. "For Arah!" he shouted in his smooth strange voice. The Sworn took it as a sign, that an abomination would speak so, and they fought on.

The second time was when the Athaji sorcerers began to attack in earnest. Crackling bolts of lightning sizzled from their fingers and burning waves of light engulfed an entire column of Sworn soldiers. The Sworn were once again ready to retreat, even though Hob and several of the Companions had beaten back the attack on their southern flank. But they steadied when Fear threw off her mantle and showed her true promise; Black serpents of writhing vapor shot from her position near where the prince had fallen; two of the Ajathi wizards were destroyed before they could even level their wards. Of the priests who still lived, many muttered to themselves "The only defense against sorcery is faith."

The third time it was Jennikar himself who steadied the army. They were falling back, many routed from the brutal attack on the northern flank. Most of the cavalry were dead or dying, and many of the Sworn nobility had been felled. Yet, upon a bloodied white charger Prince Aurum appeared again near the front. The horse seemed panicked, barely able to withstand his weight, but Aurum was alive! A horrible gash had opened his face and blood fell in slow sheets from many wounds, yet still he lived. "My people!" he cried, "To me! Rally! Rally to me!"

Again the Sworn took heart, and again the swords clashed. The Ajathi, expecting an easy battle won by work of sorcery and strategy, were forced back. Fear began to overwhelm their third sorcerer, horrible black ropes of power striking at his wards, seeking for an entrance. The Ajathi withdrew.

***

In his office of command, Prince Aurum studied Silk, the new captain of the Companions. He did not like the creature. It wrapped itself in cloth to hide whatever filth lay beneath, he knew. Its withered flesh puckered and drew back from its amber eyes. Its voice was a lying hiss, the sinuous seduction of darkness. He presented Silk with the Contract, its many coils now bundled, contained, within a huge leather tube. "Here," he said, glad to be rid of the Companions. "But do not think I will honor it to the letter."

"Prince?" the creature called Silk asked wonderingly.

"No good Sworn man will join your Companions today. I don't care how many of you were destroyed." The Prince was adamant, angry.

"I'm afraid it's too late for that, Prince Jennikar," said Silk softly.

"What!" Aurum spat. How dare this... this... thing take advantage of the chaos of battle to turn good Sworn dead into abominations like itself!

"Prince Jennikar," said Silk slowly, "the wounds you took were... almost beyond my ministrations."

Aurum touched his cheek where the gash from Mirth's knife had cut down into his jaw. He felt blood, thick and sticky, on his fingers. The world suddenly became distant as though he saw it through someone else's eyes. "What?" He asked weakly.

"Don't worry," said Silk, stepping in to support the faltering prince. Aurum tore away from him.

"Don't touch me," he whispered, staggering across the room. A brazier toppled, spilling coal and incense onto the floor. "Arah uj mah hunara," he moaned. Silk recognized it as a prayer, an imprecation. "Sun protect me from evil." The prince covered his face with one hand, tracing the ruin that he felt had been wrought there. These damn things had... killed him! "Don't think to... don't think to patronize me, creature!" he hissed.

"I would not do such a thing. I am welcoming you, Companion."

MEMENTO MORI

GARNETT ELLIOTT

Scalvi's wife, Concetta, was crawling into bed even as he thrust aside the covers. A gibbous moon the color of fresh tallow had just risen, and streamers of oily light poured in through the narrow bedroom window. Scratching, yawning, Scalvi stumbled over to look out at the nighted city of Unselmo. Orange motes flickered along the serpentine streets, where the lamp-lighters had come and gone.

Cursing his job as he did every evening, Scalvi dressed himself in doublet, hose, and shrugged on his leather cuirass, embossed at the breast with the seal of the Great Tyrant. He thrust his feet into high black boots and buckled to his head a helm thick with dark plumes. Next, he went to the armoire and drew out his equipment; truncheon, chalk, fluted pike, ring of iron keys, and most important of all, a great brass lanthorn. This he set down and filled carefully with several drams of the precious whale-oil that burned a scintillating white.

Observing him, Concetta laughed. "A night-watchman, afraid of the dark. Who could believe such a thing?"

Scalvi glowered, but continued with his work. Concetta had stripped him of all pride years before. "You might be afraid, too, if you knew what the darkness held."

"Ha. Don't think you can scare me. Your old partner, Bembo Stozzi—now there was a man. Nothing bothered him."

"Shut up about Bembo," Scalvi said, his voice thick with anger. He had long suspected his former partner of cuckoldry, though he'd been unable to prove it.

"When are they going to get you a new partner? It's dangerous out there, with just a dog."

"A requisition has been placed."

"And without gold to grease it, will likely never be filled." Concetta brushed back her graying hair to give him a concerned look. Genuine? He doubted it.

"The city works slowly," Scalvi said, "but it works."

"I left your dinner in the cook-pot."

He waved over his shoulder in a gesture that could be taken as dismissal, gratitude, or irritability—he didn't care which.

***

The moon's height suggested tardiness on Scalvi's part, so he swapped dinner for a few gulps of red wine. His dog, Goccia, waited on the stairwell. He reached down to stroke her wet nose, but she drew back, aloof. "You too, huh?" She'd been acting this way the past several weeks. Goccia's normal disposition was too sweet for a proper guard-dog, but she had the sleek white coat and dark ring around her left eye so important for Scalvi's line of work. Besides, it had made for good companionship during the lonely nights.

Together, they padded down the winding Via Crepusculo, Scalvi letting the pike-butt fall with rhythmic thumps against the flagstones. The night air reeked of fog and emptied chamber pots. He pretended he could smell the orange blossoms growing on nearby Palantino Hill, but it was simply fiction to try and raise his spirits. They passed a well-dressed prostitute leaning against a lamp post. She ignored Scalvi's greeting, keeping her eyes averted as she idly fingered the silver rings on both hands. Waiting for some lord, no doubt.

A little further, the clink of harness announced a troop of City Guard, halberds slung over their shoulders and rapiers gleaming at their belts. They gave the lone Scalvi furtive looks, some making the sign of Deus Mortis over their left breast. Scalvi paid the soldiers little heed. It had always been so; his black plumes marked him for special duty, and he accepted the stigma just as he accepted the double pay his position offered.

"They're jealous," he said aloud. "Just jealous." But that was as much fiction as the phantom orange blossoms, and he knew it.

The Via Crepusculo finally ended before a high wall of white stone, breached in the middle by an iron gate. Ancient cypress jutted beyond the wall's rim. Scalvi drew out his key-ring and unlocked the gate, before pushing it open with a tortuous creak. A glance down showed the elaborate sigils chalked across the threshold had been scuffed. Many feet must have passed through during the day, which suggested recent burials. Scalvi let out a sigh.

He stooped, and with his own chalk re-traced the complicated design, until he judged the sigils had regained their potency. Then he scraped flint against steel and got the lanthorn's wick going. Silver-white beams stabbed out over leaning headstones and a footpath choked with vines.

Goccia sniffed the air, her tail flattening against her rump. She uttered a plaintive whine.

He paused at the threshold, the sense of foreboding so thick it seemed to push at him. "I feel it too, girl." Fresh bodies stirred up trouble both within and without the cemetery walls, but it was the menace of the former that brought a chill to his gut. The Eaters of the Dead would be active. Were they watching him even now? Was that what Goccia sensed?

He gripped his pike tight and stepped inside. The gate made an ominous creak as he locked it behind him.

A low fog had come scudding down over the cypress, draping gray tendrils around the gravestones, the moon-shadowed mausoleums of hoary marble. Scalvi held the lanthorn high. Just beyond the circle of light he could discern several patches of freshly-turned earth, strewn with flowers. He counted five in all; the priests must've been busy during the day.

"Tonight we earn our coin, Goccia."

He set off on his rounds, following the path. Squeaking issued from the unkempt grass growing to either side. Mercifully, he seldom saw the huge rats that came up from the waterfront, as they'd learned to keep away from Goccia's flashing teeth. The rodents were likewise preyed upon by huge owls nesting in the cypress. On more than one occasion Scalvi had shone light into the branches above him, to behold several pairs of luminescent eyes staring down.

Tonight would've been a good night for a partner, no question. He didn't like to think too much about the hulking Bembo Stozzi, but sometimes he couldn't help it. The mind went where it went. They used to get roaring drunk, among the tombstones. Why, just over there--he shone the lanthorn at the base of a lone ash tree, long dead—they'd emptied a cask of fine Valpolicella between them, and passed out beneath the stars. Dangerous behavior, that. It was a wonder–

He halted. The faint clank of metal striking stone echoed from the wall, not thirty paces away. A low growl escaped Goccia's throat.

"Quiet, girl," he whispered, throwing down the pike. He'd heard that sound before, and knew what it signified. Out came the truncheon from his belt.

Grunts. The scrape of booted feet. Long used to peering into darkness, Scalvi could see where the three-pronged head of a grapnel had caught along the wall. A silhouette came scrambling over a moment later, to land with a quiet thud among the weeds. Then a second figure. Foregoing stealth, Scalvi whistled and pointed the lanthorn towards the pair, while his other hand brandished the truncheon. Goccia barked.

The pair of shadows didn't bolt like most intruders. Instead, they walked boldly forward, hands out at their sides. Moon and lanthorn light revealed two lanky men with grinning faces, wearing leather coats dyed midnight-black. The first had a foreigner's blond hair and a scraggly beard. The second man's face was obscured within the shadows of a gray hood. They seemed wary of the snarling Goccia, but made no move to draw weapons.

"Ah, it's just old Bembo," said the blond. "No need to get excited. We're all reasonable men, here."

Scalvi cocked the truncheon back. "Bembo disappeared some months ago. I'm his partner, Scalvi."

"That's a shame to hear. Bembo and I had an understanding." The blond nodded to his hooded companion, who, slowly, withdrew a small leather pouch and tossed it at Scalvi's feet. The pouch landed with a clink.

"What's this? A bribe?"

"We're reasonable men, as I said." The blonde's smile showed a patchwork of rotten teeth.

"We only want a single body," said the hooded man. "Fresh. The physicians at the university need corpses for their studies."

Scalvi looked down at the pouch. A little extra money was always a good thing, and these two looked dangerous. "Who am I to impede the work of scholars?" He stooped, keeping an eye on the pair while he did so.

"You see that, Salvestri? A practical man, just like Bembo." The blond laughed and reached up with his left hand as if to scratch the back of his neck.

Scalvi had seen the trick before. He threw himself to one side, just as a length of gleaming metal blurred past his ear. The blond had drawn the throwing knife from his neck-sheath and hurled it in a single motion. Scalvi called a command to Goccia; she leapt for the hooded man. He took two running steps forward and swung. His truncheon connected with the blonde's outstretched arm, making a satisfying crack. He followed up with a thrust to the belly. The blond doubled, coughing, and Scalvi saw Goccia worrying her man by the ankle. Well and good. All he had to do now was—

From behind, a weight came smashing down against the back of his helm. He pitched forward, slipping into blackness even before he struck the ground.

***

Something moist against his nose . . .

He woke with a start, expecting a multitude of grasping hands. Instead, he found only Goccia. She'd licked him then drawn away as if she hadn't liked the taste.

He was on his back. Through the cypress, he could see the moon had tracked half the sky. Out for a while, then. Raw pain throbbed from the base of his skull. The helm had probably saved his life, though it hadn't been able to stop the full force of the treacherous blow. He cursed not having a partner for the hundredth time. There must've been three body-snatchers, perhaps more, coming over the wall at a different point to sneak up on him. His ribs ached as if he'd been given a good kicking. Small wonder the robbers hadn't slit his throat.

Darkness lapped at him like a physical thing. He sat up, looking around frantically for the lanthorn. It was gone. He saw his shattered truncheon lying in the grass nearby. Someone must've snapped it over their knee. With a groan, he reached for the keys at his belt . . .

Gone as well.

"By all the bloodied saints!"

He tried to force calm, but his mind whirled at the implications. He'd locked himself inside the cemetery. He had no source of light. There was no simple way over the wall. He'd allowed the thieves to make off with at least one consecrated body. He was weaponless.

He had no source of light.

Groping along the path, his fingers touched the pike's fluted staff. They must've overlooked that. So he wasn't weaponless after all. He used the pike to steady himself as he got to his feet. Some of his old stolidness returned. Goccia limped like she'd been kicked as well, though her white fur showed no matted blood. And there was enough moonlight to at least see dimly. Not that visibility, he reminded himself, had been the lanthorn's main function. He stepped carefully down the path towards the main gate. Goccia followed several paces behind, whining. Once he'd reached the spot where the recent burials had taken place, a gaping hole told him the robbers had made good on their intent. He'd have to hide their work before daylight came. If word got back to the magistrates he'd failed in his duty, it would mean demotion and probably a suspension in pay. The predatory bureaucrats of the Great Tyrant were always seeking excuses to save money.

He looked around for a spade. The groundskeeper usually left one leaning against a mausoleum, a little further in. His head still throbbing, he groped through weeds and cypress until he caught sight of the spike-topped wall surrounding the cemetery's inner grounds. His feet shuffled to a halt.

The wall's only gate hung open.

"Goccia, come!"

He moved as fast as darkness allowed. Someone had unlocked the gate, and probably with his own key. The groundskeeper never opened it. He had good reason not to.

Several more steps and Scalvi could make out faint chalk marks across the gate's threshold. The sigils here were still intact. A good thing, though he put more trust in an iron barrier than sorcery. The thought of entering the inner grounds without a lanthorn made him shudder. On the other hand, whoever had stolen his keys could still be inside . . .

A woman's sobbing echoed faintly through the gates. A second, louder voice followed, speaking coarse words in an unknown tongue.

Scalvi's head pounded. There were people within! The prospect of revenge blotted out all instinct for self-preservation. He turned and called to Goccia, who'd halted several paces back. "Come, girl."

The dog settled on her haunches.

"I said come."

But she stayed put. No amount of cajoling or threats could bring her any closer. Scalvi threw up his hands. Goccia had always been hesitant about entering the inner grounds before, but not to the point of disobedience. He had no light; now he had no angel-eyed dog, as well. So be it. He stepped through, pulling the gate shut behind him by force of habit.

The inner section was far older than the surrounding grounds. Some whispered it was older than Unselmo itself, and had simply been expanded upon by the city's founders. Tombs of rotting marble ringed a modest knoll, with the Great Ossuary at the summit. There were no night-birds or squeaking rats to break the absolute stillness. All animal life shunned this place. Even the ancient willows here stood long dead, reaching up with skeletal branches to clutch at the moon.

He strained his ears. The sobbing was coming from the leftward path. He followed, faint will-o'-the-wisps of phosphorescent blue shimmering out the corners of his vision. The headstones here grew cruder, without adornment, for he was approaching unhallowed ground, the burial place of suicides and heretics.

The second voice joined in again. Scalvi stepped around a desiccated willow and saw where it was coming from. No further than a knife's throw away were two granite markers, flanking a rectangular slab set into the lichen-covered ground. A slender woman in a black shawl stood atop the slab. She held what looked like a wand in the crook of her arm, and had chalked some type of protective circle around herself.

Scalvi stifled a gasp. Hovering just outside the circle was a translucent figure limned with white light; a woman, dressed in tattered clothing. She'd thrown up an arm to cover her face. The black-garbed sorceress was putting questions to her in some forgotten language, and the ghost answered between sobs.

Necromancy! That he should finally witness the foul practice, after years of guarding these tombs. He might have stood transfixed through the entire rite, but his eyes caught the ring of keys hanging from the sorceress's belt. His keys.

She whirled in surprise as he charged, the wand falling from her arm to strike the slab with a metallic clank. He could see she was very young. Hair the color of fresh blood spilled down past her shoulders. At sight of Scalvi, the shade floating behind her vanished like wind-scattered smoke.

"You," he said, reaching out to seize the girl's white throat. She struck at him ineffectually before groping for her wand. Scalvi saw it was an iron rod covered with twisting symbols—perfect for braining someone senseless.

His fingers crushed the breath from her. But something made him stop. A gangrenous stench came drifting over on the night's breeze, faintly sweet—and familiar. He released his hands. A glance up showed dozens of stooped figures converging on the slab from all directions: Eaters of the Dead. Moonlight gleamed off their leprous-white flesh.

The girl drew a wracking breath. "I can explain . . ." she said, her voice trailing away as she realized the approaching danger. To her credit, she didn't scream.

Scalvi glimpsed his darkened lanthorn by her feet. "I'll forgive everything if you can get that alight, and quickly." He turned to face the shuffling, emaciated shapes.

They were close enough now that he could see them in all their scavenged finery: the tall black hats, rotting velvet capes, ebony walking-sticks, and mold-covered petticoats from previous decades. Rheumy gold jewelry flashed in the moon's glare. The once-proud clothing concealed their mortifying skin, drew attention away from the sunken ruin of their faces. Only the eyes glared with any semblance of life. Scalvi readied his pike.

A skeletal hand pointed. "We come for her . . ."

Give her to us, Scalvi."

"Let us have her."

"We want our own."

"Back!" Scalvi roared. He thrust the pike; it sheared through leather-dry flesh and struck a shoulder bone, shoving the ghoul backwards. The next moment brittle fingers closed around his ankle. He slammed the pike-butt down and shattered a wrist. Another hand reached up--

White light poured out in a radiant circle. The girl had got the lantern going, at last. A chorus of hisses arose from the ghouls as they scrabbled backwards, tripping over each other to retreat from the hateful glow.

Scalvi watched them draw back a respectful distance, though they did not disperse as he'd thought. He turned to the girl, now holding the lanthorn high. "What was all that about them wanting 'one of their own?'"

She shook her head. Her face was narrow and her dark eyes perhaps a bit too close together, but she looked beautiful all the same.

"Now's the time for answers, girl. What's your name?"

"Ysabel."

"I'm Scalvi."

"Oh, I know who you are. I've watched you many a night."

"Have you? Creeping around this place to practice necromancy, I suppose."

Her shoulders rose and fell beneath the shawl. "It's a living."

"And those two body-snatchers? Friends of yours?"

"We had a working arrangement. Unfortunately, they took fright at the prospect of penetrating further into the grounds."

"I don't blame them." Scalvi eyed the ghouls huddling just out of reach from the lanthorn's glare. As he watched, more came threading silently through the tombstones. "Something's riled these creatures tonight. Could it have anything to do with that rite you were performing?"

"I don't see why it should. I was simply asking questions for a client of mine."

"The dead have answers?"

"They have . . . a certain omniscience."

He didn't fully believe her. She must've sensed his mistrust, because she touched his arm. "The two thieves wanted to kill you, Scalvi. I talked them out of it."

"You very nearly did the job yourself. My head still aches."

"I only wanted the keys."

The well-appointed ghouls were edging closer, despite the obvious pain the light caused. Scalvi had never seen them so emboldened before. He tapped at the chalk circle with his pike. "Will this charm protect you?"

"Not from them. It's for ghosts, not creatures of flesh."

"This slab is no place to make a stand. I'd hoped to head through the gate for the outer grounds, but they're too thick in that direction."

"Where, then?"

"The hill."

He snatched the lanthorn from her hand and thrust it at a pair of ghouls who'd wriggled forward into grasping-range. The leadmost recoiled; white light seared into its ruined face just below the brim of a satin hat, causing smoke to curl. Scalvi kicked the second aside. Swinging the lanthorn before him like a censer, he broke through the enclosing ring with Ysabel tight at his heels. She swung the iron rod to good effect, snapping off a clawed hand as it reached for her.

They raced up a foot-path carved into the hillside. Shattered tombs, their doors gaping open like cave-mouths, threatened to vomit forth more of the shuffling horrors. Breathless, they reached the summit. A chorus of groans and snarls behind them bore testament to close pursuit.

"There," Scalvi said, nodding towards a squat, octagonal building of weathered gray stone. "The Great Ossuary."

"We make for that?"

"It's the most defensible building in the whole cemetery."

Ysabel voiced no further objections as they bolted for the structure. The ossuary had only a pair of doors made from bronze-sheathed timbers, and no windows. Once across the threshold, Scalvi turned and leaned his back against the doors. The lanthorn revealed row after row of stone niches, crammed with peeling brown bones. Water had seeped from the vaulted ceiling to form a shallow, musty-smelling pool at the chamber's center.

"Do you know the sigils?" Scalvi asked, reaching for the chalk tucked into his belt.

"I know many sigils. Which do you mean?"

"The kind that ward the dead."

"Well, as I explained, there are the fleshless types . . ."

The doors bucked behind Scalvi, pressing into his spine. He set his heels against the slick stone flags and pushed back. It felt like leaning against a river's inexorable current. At any moment he would go sprawling forward, and the ghouls come pouring in.

156

"Enough of this." He snatched the iron rod from her grasp and thrust it through the doors' twin handles, forming an improvised bar. Wood groaned protest, but the bar held. Scalvi stepped back and examined his handiwork.

"That just might do it," Ysabel said.

"If the hinges don't shiver loose. Draw us a magic circle proof against all dead, and don't bother me with the specifics."

"That will take hours."

"We have all night. Or at least," he gestured at the bar "for as long as that holds."

Rasping laughter echoed from the walls, from the niches, cutting off her reply. "I'm afraid you have even less time than that."

The sweat beading on Scalvi's nape went cold. He recognized that voice.

From the shadowed rear of the ossuary crept a stooped figure, its broad shoulders bowed and straining against a silk doublet tailored for a smaller man. Muscles hung like slack ropes down its long arms, the flesh no longer pliant. It wore a worm-eaten cloak of black velvet, a broad-brimmed hat, and a silver chain with a dangling snuff box. The figure stopped short of the lanthorn's light and lifted its head. Scalvi took a gulping breath.

"Bembo," he said.

The creature that had once been Bembo Stozzi doffed the hat and bowed low, revealing lank black hair going bone-white at the tips. "Good to see you again, Scalvi. If you don't mind, would you please shutter your lanthorn a bit? It hurts my eyes."

Scalvi stooped to comply out of habit, and then stopped himself. "What happened to you? You disappeared . . ."

"All will be explained, old friend. But the light first. Please."

"Don't do it," Ysabel said.

Bembo's withered lips parted in a smile as he turned to her. "Ah. A young lady. And one of our own, too."

"What are you talking about?" Ysabel said. If Bembo's appearance unsettled her, she didn't show it.

"Can it be? Is it possible that you, of all people, fail to grasp what's been happening? I've watched you, flame-hair, just as you've watched Scalvi, skulking around the headstones and calling up decrepit spirits. You're a necromancer. No doubt the practice of your art has accelerated the change."

"What change?" Scalvi said.

"You'll recall that I'd been watching the grounds for two years before you signed on. So I've had more exposure." Bembo leaned over the stagnant pool to observe his own reflection. He tittered and drew back. "It's the night that does it, Scalvi. Living as we do, shunning the daylight, breathing in all the unwholesome vapors of decay . . ."

"You're saying we're turning into them?" Ysabel pointed a trembling hand towards the doors, where soft moans could still be heard.

"One acquires the moon-pallor, first," Bembo went on. "Then the appetite wanes. Animals become nervous, in our presence, and sunlight a little too strong for the eyes. By degrees the physical manifestation sets in, though the mind succumbs faster."

Scalvi licked his lips. Hadn't Goccia been treating him strangely? And for the past few days he'd eaten little of Concetta's cooking, subsisting instead on red wine. Worse, there'd been a malaise he'd attributed to simple melancholy. "Can you prove any of this, Bembo?" he said, trying to marshal his reason. "Why should we believe all your mad talk of transformation?"

"See for yourself." Bembo gestured with wizened fingers at the lanthorn. "Examine the girl. Closely."

Wary of a ruse, Scalvi took up the lanthorn and shone it over Ysabel's face, careful to shield the glare from her eyes. The bright light revealed details the moon had spared. Her skin looked so pale as to be translucent, with a faint web-work of blue veins running underneath.

"What do you see?" Ysabel said.

"Nothing." He set the lanthorn back down. "You're very fair-complexioned, is all."

Bembo laughed. "That's not all, Scalvi. Why do you deny it?"

"You're having sport with us."

"With my old partner?" Bembo's grin showed rotten gums hanging in black shreds. "Our howling brethren outside aren't interested in 'sport.' They want the girl, as I'm sure they've told you."

"They want to devour her, you mean."

"For good reason. This cemetery's grown crowded over the years.

Not enough space for all our Lords and Ladies of the night, and certainly not enough food. They're aware this girl's close to turning; they can smell it. Consuming her now keeps the population in check."

"And how do you know all this?"

"Because they tried to do it to me."

"Don't listen to him, Scalvi," Ysabel said. "Spear the filthy thing, and be done."

Bembo shook his head. "I've got a better idea. Let me kill the girl, and give her to the ghouls outside. They're not interested in you, Scalvi. Yet. I can persuade them to leave you alone."

"That sounds barbaric."

"It's your best chance. And for you, sweet girl, a knife-thrust is cleaner than being torn limb from limb." Bembo draped the velvet cloak over part of his face, shielding him from the light. He reached for the hem of Ysabel's shawl. She cried out and stepped behind Scalvi, who shoved his former friend backwards.

"What's this?" Bembo said, recovering his balance. "You never let a woman get between us before. Why, as I recall, you were downright gracious when I sampled that little vixen, Concetta–"

"Hold your rotten tongue." Scalvi raised the pike.

In response, Bembo reached beneath his doublet and drew a vicious poniard. The blade hadn't left its sheath before Scalvi thrust forward, the pike's iron head piercing through silk to flesh itself in Bembo's chest. Scalvi gave a shout of triumph. But Bembo didn't cry out, didn't wince, merely looked down at the length of wooden shaft protruding from his body and snapped it off clean with a flick of his hand. Shielding his face as before, he slashed at Scalvi. The watchman threw himself back as the poniard cut through his leather cuirass and scored the skin along his stomach. Any deeper, and the stroke would've disemboweled him.

Bembo barked laughter. He readied the knife to thrust at the defenseless Scalvi, who'd backed himself against the ossuary doors.

But in the next moment, the lanthorn came sailing through the air. It struck Bembo just above the sundered pike and shattered into a hundred fragments, spilling burning whale-oil over the silk and velvet finery. This time, Bembo did cry out. He screamed as orange flames licked him from neck to waist. First his lank hair caught, next the hat, and the ossuary filled with an acrid stench. He tried to beat out the fire with frantic blows, but the dry flesh of his hands burned as well. Bembo Stozzi dropped to the flags. Mewling, he crawled towards the nearby pool of dank water.

Scalvi reached out and grabbed a smoldering ankle. Bembo tried to claw his way forward, to no avail. The flames rose higher as the rest of his body burned like a torch. Scalvi was forced to let go. After several long moments, Bembo no longer twitched.

The flames glowed red and died, plunging the ossuary into total darkness.

Outside, countless hands scratched at the doors.

***

When morning light at last seeped past the doorjambs, an exhausted Scalvi drew the iron rod free and threw open the portals. The night's fog had burned away. Blinking, he stepped outside. Clawed fingers had gouged nearly halfway through the door's exterior.

"It's safe," he called to Ysabel.

She came shuffling towards the doorway, but flinched when sunlight touched her face. "It's too bright."

"Give your eyes a moment to adjust."

"They're not going to adjust, Scalvi." She withdrew deeper into the shadows, the black shawl striking a wraith-like contrast against her pale skin. "What your friend said is true."

"That was just him trying to trick–"

"No. No tricks. I know it, now. And . . . I'm comfortable, here."

Absently, as if she was unaware of the gesture, her left hand floated up to a niche and stroked the contours of the skull within.

"I'm taking you from this place." Scalvi stepped back inside, intending to haul her out by force, if necessary. But when he leaned close she seized his face between her hands and kissed him. Scalvi stood transfixed. If her lips felt a trifle cool, the pressure of her fingertips somewhat clammy, he scarce took notice. After a long moment he had to break away, gasping.

"I'm staying here," she said. "Come back and see me tonight. I'll wait for you."

"But the ghouls . . ."

160

"I can hide from them as Bembo did."

He shook his head. "I won't return. I'll quit the Guard and take my wife to some city in the north, far from any graveyards. The sickness Bembo spoke of will fail to claim me."

"Tonight, Scalvi," Ysabel whispered. "Now go."

She closed the ossuary doors behind him.

THE VIVISECTIONIST'S TALE

SEAN P. ROBSON

Avram al'Zuul was a self-styled scholar and, depending on the needs of his customers, a butcher, a barber, and a chirurgeon. He lived and worked out of his shop on Mourner's Row, cutting hair and patients in the front room; meat and cadavers in the back. His location in the district of Death Gate, adjacent to the necropolis, made it easy for Avram to obtain cadavers, and for his patient's next-of-kin to make funeral arrangements.

Owing to the late hours he kept and the obsessive single-mindedness with which he pursued his studies, Avram was habitually over-tired and underfed, to the point where he was beginning to look cadaverous himself. Indeed, it was with some concern that his neighbors remarked upon his pale, gaunt face and dark rings that encircled his sunken eyes. Several local widows with a mind for marriage—for Avram's three vocations afforded him a comfortable albeit modest income—had taken to delivering fresh-baked pies and pastries to Avram's shop. But the pies, more often than not, lay forgotten and untouched except by the rats, which were looking not at all gaunt.

The practice of chirurgery requires a steady supply of cadavers to study, and when the Vizier's barrow wardens started cracking down on tomb-robbers and body-snatchers, the price of corpses soared so high that Avram was forced to create his own. One night each week, he haunted the tenement district of Hope's End, which was rarely patrolled by the city watch, and rife with inhabitants that no one would miss. He prowled its narrow, labyrinthine alleyways with his pomander held close to his face to ward against the reek of tannery fumes, human waste, and despair, in search of a drunken derelict or unwary whore, whom he would lure back to his workshop with the promise of a friendly drink or a quick tumble. Then, with a paternal embrace, he would slide his needle-sharp awl between the joints of their cervical vertebrae and they'd drop like puppets with their strings cut—alive but paralyzed. For a time, their hearts continued to beat, lungs to expand, and blood to flow, and they taught him more about the human body and how it worked than his more scrupulous colleagues could learn in years of practice.

Late one night, while hunting in Hope's End, Avram spied a suitable subject stumbling down a deserted alley oblivious to her surroundings—probably an akla addict. Akla, derived from the hallucinogenic venom of a dreamweaver spider, was a potent narcotic and, for many of Catapesh's indigent citizens, a popular respite from the cruel indifference of daily life. The woman offered not the least resistance as Avram carefully guided her over cobble-stone streets, through alleyways and down avenues, and finally to his shop.

Avram shoved his awl into the back of her neck and was surprised when, instead of collapsing paralyzed to the floor, she continued to shuffle slowly about the shop in remarkable defiance of the five-inch steel spike embedded in her nervous system.

Intrigued and confused, he hoisted the woman onto his operating table and tied her down before she could climb off. He cut off her dress with a pair of barber's shears then pricked her several times with the point of his awl. No response. Next he picked up a sharp boning knife and cut through her abdominal wall, opening it up for examination. All the while his subject showed no awareness, whatsoever, of the trauma being inflicted, and she turned her head to and fro looking around the workshop, oblivious to the proceedings.

He then cut off the top of the woman's skull with a bone saw, to examine her brain, and recoiled in shock to find the grey matter riddled through with fungal hyphae. There was little healthy brain tissue left and most of the brain case was now infested by a fibrous mass of mycelium. How she still lived, Avram did not know, but he traced the parasitic infection through her brain stem and down the entire length of her nerve cord. The fungus appeared to have taken over her nervous system, keeping her alive but insensate. This presented some intriguing possibilities.

For several days Avram kept the woman bound to his workbench.

He fed her a thin pottage of oats and pork thrice daily with plenty of water. She respired, ate, digested, and excreted while Avram opened her up; the knowledge he gained in those first few days was incalculable, and he'd only begun to plumb her depths. On the evening of the fourth day, however, he threw off her cover sheet to find her dead with lurid red and purple spheres—putrid spore-filled puffballs—erupting from her ears, nose and eye sockets.

Avram carefully harvested the puffballs, and stored them in his cool, dark cellar. He was excited by the opportunities this strange fungus afforded him—he had within his grasp the means to become the most skilled chirurgeon Catapesh had ever known. The cost would be terrible, yes, but well worth it; soon he would be able to treat ailments that lesser men believed were incurable.

At least this is what he boasted to his friend and putative colleague, Callum Bajere, whose hair he was cutting late one afternoon. Bajere was a lecturer and fellow of the College of Healers and he regarded mere chirurgeons with the condescending disregard of professional for layman, which galled Avram and prompted his boastful remarks.

"Now Avram," said Bajere, "I don't disparage your skill with a knife. If it's a cut of meat for my dinner that I want, you're the first man I'll turn to. But until you manage to save more people than you kill on your operating table I'll put my faith in my leeches."

"And faith is exactly what you practice," said Avram. "You and your fellows at the college dogmatically adhere to treatments based not on observation of cause and effect, nor on any understanding of human biology, but on traditions sanctioned by priests who know nothing of the natural world. You of the college, with your incenses, herbs, and chants don't practice science, you peddle superstition."

"Ah, yes, your infamous experiments," Bajere replied, "We've all heard tales of how you cut up cadavers in defiance of ecclesiastic decree. The desecration of the dead is proscribed by the Gods, Avram; how long do you think you can carry on without drawing the attention of the templars? If you want my advice, my friend, leave healing to the Healers and stick to what you are good at." Bajere examined himself in a looking glass. "A little more off the top if you don't mind."

Avram seethed with frustration, but he knew that Callum was right. Without an influential patron he, Avram al'Zuul, might well be branded a heretic and hauled before an ecclesiastical court, and he harbored no illusions of mercy—not for an avowed atheist such as himself.

The patronage that Avram sought came in the unlikely form of the Vizier, whose favorite concubine, Yasmeena, was with child and near to term. Her three previous pregnancies had ended in still-births despite the attendance of Healers and priests. The last time, she not only lost the child, but nearly died herself, despite four successive blood-lettings during the delivery. The Vizier was anxious to save this baby, who augurs had foretold would be a son—his first—and he was prepared to take the unorthodox measure of consulting a chirurgeon despite protests from the College and Church.

With equal measures of excitement and trepidation, Avram answered the summons and was escorted into the Vizier's audience chamber, flanked by a guardsman on either side. While the Overlord was the titular ruler of Catapesh, the Vizier, who oversaw the administration of the city, was truly in charge. Thus, he was constantly surrounded by obsequious functionaries and sycophants who competed to curry favor with His Greatness; among them, a trio of priests who hissed with displeasure upon Avram's arrival.

"Greatness, we implore you, send this butcher away," said one of the priests, craning his neck towards the Vizier like a vulture, "he is uncouth and unworthy of the honor you show him."

"Indeed, Greatness," added a second priest, spreading his hands in supplication, "this unwashed hog-gutter is a mere dabbler; he is unsanctioned by the College of Healers."

"He is not favored by the Gods," said the third, stroking his oiled beard. "Call for a Healer and cast this charlatan out, unless it is a haircut you desire."

"Enough!" said the Vizier, slapping the arm of his chair, "neither Healers, nor Gods have given me a living son; I will speak with this chirurgeon. Now be gone, all of you." He waved his arm to encompass the entire chamber and the attendant functionaries began to scuttle out of the room, fussing over their abrupt dismissal. The guardsmen, Avram noted, remained.

The Vizier rose from his chair and walked slowly across the hall toward Avram, transfixing him with a raptor-sharp gaze. The two men said nothing for several moments; each studying the other. The

Vizier had a palpable sense of self-possession and Avram sensed that he was not the sort of man to bluster or prevaricate; he would say what he meant and expect the same of others.

"Master al'Zuul, I've heard that you have pioneered new frontiers in the field of chirurgery, and enjoyed success far beyond that of your fellows."

Avram inclined his head in acknowledgement. "I have, Greatness," he said. Heard from whom? Rumors of his studies abounded, but they were seldom favorable, and no one with the Vizier's ear was likely to extol the virtues of Avram al'Zuul.

"How have you achieved these advances? How have you learned that which has eluded so many others," said the Vizier.

"The body is but a machine that houses the soul," said Avram. "When a machine breaks it can be mended, but only if we know how it works; how all the various components function as part of the whole. I started by studying the bodies of pigs, which are not very different from our own." Avram faltered here; it was usually unwise to point out to wealthy and powerful rulers their similarity to swine. He paused briefly, hoping that his assessment of the Vizier was correct, and then pressed on.

"But to truly understand the human body, I needed to open it up and find out how it worked. I needed to dissect human cadavers, not pigs, to further my studies and this is why I have achieved greater success than most chirurgeons—I do not operate blindly and hope for the best, I know exactly where to cut and how deeply, and how to mend what is broken."

"So, you are a heretic," said the Vizier.

Avram said nothing.

"Well the Gods have done me no favors," said the Vizier. "If you can deliver me a living son the priests and their proscriptions can be damned. Can you?"

"Complications can arise that no man—nor apparently the Gods—can foresee, and I will know more once I have examined the Lady Yasmeena, but given her previous difficulties in labor the safest option is to cut the baby from her womb. I can assure you in all humility that I am the most capable man in all of Catapesh to perform this procedure." Avram projected an outward appearance of confidence, but on the inside his stomach was churning and his heart was racing. His future hung in the balance and the Vizier held the scales. If Avram saved the Vizier's son and concubine he would gain the favor of the most powerful man in Catapesh; if he failed he would be damned—a confessed heretic.

Seconds seemed to drag into hours before the Vizier nodded, ending Avram's torment. "So be it, Chirurgeon," the Vizier said. "You shall have your chance. If you succeed you will be richly rewarded." The rest was left unspoken.

***

Three days later the Vizier had a son named Uksem and Avram had a powerful and grateful patron, who promptly appointed him to the newly-founded position of Master Chirurgeon to the Overlord's Court. The story of Uksem's delivery was recounted by the many courtiers who hadn't witnessed it, and, with each telling, the legend of the Master Chirurgeon grew so that within a week popular rumor had it that Avram had brought the still-born babe back from the dead.

In truth, the operation had been routine and so straightforward that it might have been performed by any chirurgeon in Catapesh, for which Avram was profoundly grateful, though he did nothing to dispel the exaggerated rumors of his miraculous achievement. More remarkable was Yasmeena's recovery. Other chirurgeons before Avram had cut a baby from the womb, but had always killed the mother in the process. Avram had worked with surety, completing the operation in only a few minutes, and kept Yasmeena's bleeding to a minimum. Moreover, her flesh showed no sign of mortification; it would heal cleanly and she would live to raise her son.

Avram spent most of the Vizier's largesse establishing a shelter and soup-kitchen in Hope's End where the indigent could get a free meal, akla addicts could ride out their hallucinations in safety, and Avram could obtain living subjects for dissection without having to wander dangerous alleys in the dead of night. This act of apparent philanthropy further elevated the Master Chirurgeon's growing reputation, especially among the common folk.

Ironically, however, Avram's success won him more enemies than friends. He had demonstrated the efficacy of chirurgery, and it now posed a serious threat to the primacy of the College of Healers— one that they could not afford to ignore. There were also all the courtiers and the scions of wealthy families who were jealous of Avram's rapid ascent. He had risen from obscurity to city-wide celebrity almost overnight, and the influence and respect he had garnered so quickly was ill-regarded by those who had spent years currying favor at court. All of this, and more, was pointed out to him by Callum Bajere, who was disappointed to find that Avram no longer had either the time or inclination to cut his hair.

"I suppose congratulations are in order," Bajere said, blowing an errant forelock out of his eyes. "You are the talk of the College."

"Oh, yes?" Avram smirked. He'd expected the College to capitulate and offer him a fellowship; he'd even envisioned establishing chirurgery as a school in the College, with himself as its dean.

"Indeed," Bajere replied. "Though, in truth, the debate is whether to include you in our ranks or have you killed, so perhaps congratulations are premature."

***

Avram affected an air of indifference to Bajere's revelation but, in truth, he was stung by the College's intransigence. He should have known they would balk at innovation—the archconservative cabalists hadn't revised their practices in over two centuries. Small wonder they'd failed to recognize a visionary in their midst. So be it. He would found his own school and supplant the College. Hidden in his shop he had the means to consign the College of Healers to obsolescence.

Thus committed, Avram embarked upon the plan that had taken root the day he'd harvested the fungal fruit from the dead woman. The embryonic idea had festered in the weeks since and grown ripe. Retrieving one of the puffballs from the cellar in his workshop, Avram harvested its spores and germinated them in rye bread bound for his soup kitchen.

He distributed the infested loaves personally, handing them out to select lone subjects who resided at the boarding house. He had a moment's misgiving when one of the men shared his bread with a young child, but quickly overcame it: this was for the greater good.

Avram was approached by a middle-aged man in torn, soiled robes that stank of dried sweat, stale urine, and cheap wine. "My name's Djabar," he said, with tears in his eyes. He grasped Avram's hand and squeezed it. "Can't thank you enough for what you done for us, Master al'Zuul. Don't remember the last roof that covered my head, nor a bite I didn't have to fight a rat for. You're a good man, sir."

"It is my sincere pleasure," said Avram. He patted Djabar on the shoulder, deeply touched by the man's heartfelt gratitude. "Here, have some bread."

And so it went: desperate mothers, infirm grandfathers, hopeless addicts—all the detritus of Hope's End—came to partake of Avram's benevolence. Meanwhile, Avram's star continued to rise: he was able to move to the fashionable neighborhood of Sea View and set up a clinic where he counted some of Catapesh's finest citizens among his clientele. He lanced a boil on the right buttock of Ladislaus Dragomere, commander of the barrow wardens; treated Hamdi al' Bashir, a prosperous vintner, for gout; and frequently relieved Lady Siona of House Torenescu of her female hysteria. Such minor maladies could have been treated by any mere barber, but it was now a mark of prestige to be seen to by the Master Chirurgeon, himself.

The steady flow of wealthy patrons afforded Avram sufficient prosperity that he no longer needed the copper pittance paid by low-born patients. Wealth and affluence meant far less to him, however, than establishing his own College of Chirurgeons, and the flotsam of Hope's End were the means to that goal. So he spent part of each day at his soup kitchen, distributing his bread to the destitute and treating their ailments. He watched and he waited, and within five days the first subjects began to show signs of infection.

Djabar lined up for breakfast one morning looking peaked and wan. Avram, who had been keeping close watch on the infected subjects, asked Djabar what ailed him.

"It's nothin," Djabar mumbled. "Just et somethin that wants back out; got a touch of the flux, and I bin tossin up pretty regular." He paused and touched his temple. "My head's painin me, too, but no worse than many a mornin after."

"And you've not been over-indulging in spirits?"

"Ain't touched a drop since I came here, sir. I'm turnin a new page and cleanin up my life," said Djabar. "Sides, I ain't got two coins to rub together, anyhow."

"I'm sure it's nothing to worry about," said Avram. "But...just to be on the safe side has anyone else been feeling unwell?"

"Well, old Hedda's bin havin spasms, crampin up somethin awful, but I guess that's what comes of gettin on, as she is. An that young fella, Kenan," Djabar pointed to a sallow-skinned boy of twelve, who was standing in a corner muttering to himself and scratching his arms furiously. "He's had a bout a the flux, same as me, an it looks like the bed bugs have bin at him."

Djabar twitched then started scratching his leg. "Heh; guess they bin at me, too."

One by one all the subjects who ate Avram's tainted bread began to show the symptoms described by Djabar: headaches, nausea, diarrhea, itching, and painful spasms. But the strangest symptoms of all did not appear until three days later, and at the worst possible time.

The Lady Yasmeena, now fully recovered from her operation, had heard of Avram's charitable work in the tenement district, and she wished to tour his boarding house and soup kitchen. A favorable review to her Lord husband—so pleased was the Vizier with the birth of his son that he'd married her—might secure permanent funding for the facility. It was a chance that Avram could not pass up, and so he hastened to the soup kitchen ahead of her arrival to make certain that everything was ship-shape. He found it in a state of bedlam.

Amid screams of panic, Avram pushed his way against the tide of people rushing for the exit and saw two of his subjects upend a cauldron of scalding-hot soup over their own heads; three more danced on tables in various states of undress. Hedda and Djabar were fornicating, naked, atop a pile of bread loaves, the old woman's sagging, blue-veined breasts flouncing with wild abandon as she rode him with the vigor of a woman a third her age. Avram's attention was so unwillingly riveted to the grotesque scene that he almost missed the most horrific thing of all—that which drove the other patrons from the hall: young Kenan sat quietly in the corner, a butcher knife in hand, gnawing on a heart he had just cut from the chest of a young girl who lay dead before him in a expanding pool of blood.

"No!" Avram's cry of anguish silenced the din. "Stop it! Stop it now! You can't..." He looked around desperately, and spied the cook cowering behind a wood-stove. He gestured to Kenan in the corner.

"Get him out of here, and clean up this mess."

The cook peered over the stove at the bloody boy across the room. "I ain't touchin him," he said.

Avram ran a hand through his hair in frustration. "Well, then get these two sorted out and get them dressed," he said, jabbing a finger at Hedda and Djabar.

"Ain't touchin them, neither," the cook muttered.

But by then Djabar had spent himself and Hedda climbed off, ogling Avram with a sparkle of lust in her cataract-misted eyes. "Damn it, man, just do it—and quickly," Avram ordered. He then advanced cautiously towards Kenan. The boy growled like a jackal and held the half-eaten heart protectively against his chest.

"Just calm down, boy, and give me the knife," said Avram in as soothing a voice as he could manage. He stepped closer and held out his hand.

Kenan howled in rage and hurled himself at Avram, slashing wildly. Avram jumped back, narrowly avoiding the blade, which sliced a rent in his shirt. He tripped over the outstretched arm of the corpse and fell. Kenan landed on top of him, stabbing viciously at Avram's head. Avram grabbed the boy's wrist with both hands, and the two grappled desperately for possession of the knife, rolling in the blood and over the body of the dead girl.

Meanwhile the cook, holding a blanket to wrap her in, was tripping and stumbling after Hedda, who pranced naked between the overturned tables and chairs. Djabar was doubled over, grunting, cock in hand, attempting to coax another erection for a second go with the old woman.

It was at this unhappy juncture that the Lady Yasmeena and her entourage arrived. Avram, who had finally succeeded in wresting the blade away from Kenan, stood up panting, covered in gore, holding the dripping butcher knife. He tried to explain himself, and reassure her ladyship that all was under control, but this was belied by his appearance, the equally bloody boy snarling next to him, and the body of the dead girl at their feet. To make matters worse, Hedda was hooting with pleasure, thrusting her crotch at the new arrivals, and running her hands suggestively over her flabby belly and breasts, while Djabar, successful in his endeavors, strutted toward Yasmeena, his manhood jutting proudly.

Yasmeena and her ladies shrieked and fled, while her guards drew swords and backed out of the building. Avram stumbled after them, still trying to salvage the situation.

"Come back! My lady, it's not as it seems. Lunatics; just a couple of lunatics wreaking havoc, but we've got it all under control now. Please, you must understand!" Avram left off when one of the guards leveled a sword at his chest and shook his head. What an unmitigated disaster. Word of this would spread through the court faster than fire through a cotton mill; he would be a laughing stock.

***

The soup kitchen was finished. Even the rough-and-tumble residents of Hope's End, who were so inured to violence that their only concern when seeing a corpse was whether it had already been looted, now shunned the place. The Hope's Enders didn't fear such a familiar companion as death, but the soup kitchen was attainted by rumors of madness and sorcery, and that they did fear. Now, instead of stopping in to warm themselves and have a bite, they spat and traced the symbol of Heka over their hearts to ward off evil spirits as they passed by.

Avram salvaged what he could. Many of the infected subjects had wandered off, unobserved, during the chaos that ruined his operation in Hope's End, but he'd managed to move several of them, including Djabar, Hedda, and Kenan to his old shop on Mourner's Row. They'd become so uncontrollable that they now needed to be kept in restraint, tied to their beds at all times. Djabar, in obvious agony, moaned and cried incessantly; Hedda thrashed so violently that her wrists and ankles were a bloody ruin from straining at her ropes; Kenan, however, had become unresponsive. Avram thought that he was now ready for dissection. It was seven days since Kenan's initial infection. In four more, Avram would probably be harvesting mushrooms from his corpse.

As predicted, business at his Sea View clinic dwindled after the soup kitchen incident, and he learned that a reputation founded solely on rumor cut both ways, though he was far less willing to let this new one stand. The popular account of what folk were calling 'the Hope's End Massacre' was greatly exaggerated and grew wilder with each telling.

He'd even heard that he, Avram al'Zuul, led a cult of demon-worshipers that befouled the dead in orgiastic rituals. His attempts to gain an audience with the Vizier and explain himself were rebuffed by stony-faced guards, and he was shunned by the people who had so recently courted him.

Avram was dismayed by his sudden reversal of fortune, and he gratefully accepted an invitation to dine with Callum Bajere at his Sea View estate. He looked forward to having someone to talk to, even though the invitation was probably just an excuse for Bajere, who seldom passed up an opportunity to gloat, to rub Avram's nose in his plight. Much to his surprise, however, Bajere was uncharacteristically solicitous. He commiserated with Avram, providing a sympathetic ear and an ever full wineglass. But secrets and alcohol are bad bedfellows as Avram, an ascetic by habit and unaccustomed to drink, discovered to his lasting regret.

"It is a shame that things turned out as they did," said Bajere. He belched, and pushed away his plate, which still held a few uneaten pork medallions—the wine reduction wasn't quite to his liking. "But you must look at things from the larger perspective. You've may have suffered an irreparable blow to your reputation, but the practice of chirurgery will spread, nonetheless."

"Yes, I suppose that is true," said Avram. He toyed with the food on his own plate, too preoccupied to enjoy it. He raised his glass to drink, found it empty again, and waggled it at the servant holding the decanter. "I'll continue with my studies, of course, but do you really believe I can make up the ground I've lost and regain the trust of the city?"

"No, but that isn't what I meant. The College has decided to found a school of chirurgery."

"Truly?" Avram's eyes lit up and he smiled for the first time in days. "That's incredible news! Why did you wait until after supper to tell me?" He quaffed his glass of wine with gusto and gestured to the servant again. "When am I to be invested?"

"Er...you aren't." Bajere looked uncomfortable. "I've been promoted to the rank of deacon and appointed as dean of the new school. I'm to superintend the integration of chirurgery into the College's practice."

Avram's heart froze in his chest and his stomach plummeted; he couldn't be hearing this correctly. After a few seconds the shock of his betrayal melted in a blaze of apoplexy. "How can you do this to me, Bajere: I trusted you," he bellowed, his face flushed with anger and too much wine.

"Be reasonable, Avram. You're too erratic and you've made too many enemies within the College and the priesthood. You are a maverick and you have practiced heresy in the pursuit of your studies. Honestly, did you ever truly believe you would be accepted as one of us?"

Avram snorted. "Just how do you expect to study chirurgery without engaging in the very same heresies? Without an intimate understanding of human anatomy, you'll do no better than a common barber."

"Dispensations for dissection can be granted to anointed members of the College: practitioners who are sanctioned by the gods. In a way, you've brought this on yourself. When I recommended you to the Vizier, I fully expected you'd botch the job and we'd be done with all this chirurgery nonsense. Then you could carry on with your proper calling, and I with mine."

"You recommended? You set me up to fail?" Avram stared, stunned. "You put the Vizier's concubine and child at risk simply to discredit me?"

"Yes, but the risk was low; there were Healers waiting nearby to step in when you failed." Bajere shrugged. "But, contrary to all expectations, you succeeded famously, and now there is no putting the djinni back in its bottle. We at the College realized we'd need to adapt to the times, and with the help of your notes, I'm sure that I will be able to match your achievements, and, given my superior medical training, soon surpass them."

"You have the gall to usurp me and then ask me for my notes? You must be mad, Bajere, if you think I'll help you. Besides, without living subjects to work on, you'll never –" Avram cut off suddenly, inwardly cursing his wine-loosened tongue and befuddled wit.

Bajere's eyes narrowed for a moment, then widened in understanding. "So the rumors were true." He shrugged. "Nonetheless, while your cooperation would be helpful, it isn't necessary. We obtained a writ from the Vizier—Lady Yasmeena still hasn't recovered from the shock of visiting you. Temple guards have already been dispatched to your Sea View clinic. They'll confiscate whatever notes you have there; then at Mourner's Row, and Hope's End."

Mourner's Row. Djabar, Hedda, and the others were still tied to their beds, along with Kenan, who lay writhing upon the operating table, spread open like a butterflied fish. Avram bolted from the table. He ran full-tilt into a servant, who was coming into the dining room carrying a tea service. The teapot, along with cream, honey, and the servant, crashed to the floor. Avram nearly followed them to the ground, but he managed to keep his feet; he caromed off the door jam, then righted himself and fled out of the house and into the street.

He looked around frantically for a cab, and spotted a horse-drawn araba that was rounding a corner and headed away. He chased after it, waving his arms and yelling for the driver to stop. When he caught up with it, Avram hauled a man from the passenger's seat dumping him onto the street, and then climbed into the carriage, ignoring the protests of both the driver and the furious passenger on the ground. Avram pressed three talents of gold into the driver's hand; more than enough to convince him to leave his former fare where he lay.

"Mourner's Row, as fast as you can go," Avram said, jingling his coin purse for incentive. The driver applied whip to horse and the araba was soon hurtling from the heights of Sea View down towards Death Gate like an avalanche. The cab bounced over the cobblestone streets, jarring Avram's bones and rattling his teeth, and he hung tight, fearing that the carriage would shake itself apart. It didn't, although when the driver finally reined the horses in outside of Avram's shop on Mourner's Row, he felt as beaten as a rug on cleaning day. He wasted no time recovering, though, and he flung himself from the carriage the moment it stopped, tossing more coins over his shoulder at the driver as he sprinted for the door.

He eased the door open and stuck his head inside. All was quiet and dark. Thank the gods—he had arrived in time! He lit an oil lamp, then hurried to the back room and retrieved his research journal from his desk drawer. He tucked the book into his coat pocket, and then went to the cellar to collect the remaining puffballs, which he gently deposited in a cloth sack. He would need these to resume his research, though perhaps not in Catapesh; he had enough money left to begin anew in another city—perhaps Kashpur.

He grabbed a flask of lamp oil on his way out of the cellar, and then emptied it all over his workshop, taking care to liberally douse his test subjects. It had been a close call: the College nearly bested him, but now he was safe. Only the shop on Mourner's Row contained anything that could help them—or incriminate him. He had what he needed. The rest would go up in flames along with Bajere's dreams of stolen glory.

Just as Avram was emptying the last of the flask onto Djabar's moaning face, he heard a commotion from the front of the shop. They were here. Gods be damned, why could the meddlesome buggers not have come just a few minutes later? He hid behind the door to the back room and sheltered the lamp within his coat, casting the room into darkness. Voices in the front of the shop became louder as a party of men approached. The first of the temple guards entered the back room, holding a flickering torch before him making shadows dance on the walls. The guard saw the victims tied down on the beds, and heard Djabar who was spitting and coughing up lamp oil. He called his fellows, and Avram waited quietly until they were all in the back room with him, untying his subjects. One of them uttered an oath and made the sign of Heka when he spotted Kenan, his intestines spilling from his abdomen, his chest cavity cracked wide open, still struggling feebly against his restraints.

Avram stepped out from behind the door and hurled his lamp to the floor at the guards' feet. The flames quickly spread across the pool of oil, and the men cried out in alarm. Taking advantage of the confusion, he dashed out the door and through the front room only to find the exit blocked by a burly, mail-clad sergeant who was just entering the building. Desperate, Avram lowered his head and charged into the guardsman, catching him by surprise and knocking him back through the doorway. Avram stumbled into the street, off balance from the impact, and trying to get his feet back under him. He slipped on a loose cobble and pitched headlong to the ground, landing heavily on his sack. A brown cloud of spores erupted from the burst puffballs, and Avram coughed, and then covered his mouth and nose with his sleeve. He was half-way to his feet and already moving forward when he felt a mail gauntlet grasp the collar of his coat, then another on his arm. He struggled furiously to break free and lose himself in the twisting streets of Death Gate. He was so close; he could taste freedom in the night air, but he was held fast in the sergeant's iron grip then shaken like a rat in a terrier's jaws.

Avram ceased his struggles. He was caught. His spores were gone, evaporating into the night along with his hope. He sagged, resigned, and the fight went out of him. He offered the guards no further resistance as they took him into custody.

Avram's trial was short, and the outcome was unsurprising. A full account of his experiments was recorded in his journal, and the temple guards had put out the fire in his shop before the flames reached his test subjects. There was no possible defense against the evidence brought against him, and the horror of it shocked even the most jaded members of the court. He was found guilty and sentenced to death.

From the barred window of his cell overlooking the Plaza of Infinite Regret, Avram could see the headsman's block that awaited him. He was still unable to make himself believe that this was really happening. He had acted with the best of intentions, for the betterment of all mankind. What was the sacrifice of a few homeless people compared to that? Scores of them died everyday from starvation, disease, or violence. Avram gave their lives and their death meaning. Surely Djabar, at least, would understand that.

Avram had finally resolved himself to his fate when he had a moment of renewed hope in the form of a visit by Callum Bajere. He reached through the bars on his door and grasped the Healer's lapels. "Bajere! You've got to help me. You can explain everything; you can make them understand."

"I'm sorry, Avram." Bajere shook his head. He looked sad. "If only you had cooperated, this would never have happened. You were too proud to bend, so now you are broken."

Bajere pried Avram's fingers off his coat and stepped back out of reach. "Would it comfort you to know that you may still make a contribution to the field you have so greatly advanced," Bajere asked.

"How can I," said Avram, "locked in this cell and awaiting the headsman?"

"There has been an amendment to ecclesiastic law: henceforth, the bodies of executed felons will be delivered to the College of Healers for dissection." Bajere smiled sadly. "Goodbye, Avram. You won't see me again, but I'll soon see you."

178

Bajere turned and left. The strength drained from Avram's legs. He slumped to the floor, sobbing, and massaged his throbbing temples. He felt suddenly nauseated, lunged for the night-soil bucket, and heaved up his breakfast. As he recognized the signs, Avram began to laugh hysterically. He sat on the straw-strewn floor of his cell with vomit dripping from his chin, and for the first and last time in his life, he prayed to the gods although he knew they would not listen.

CONTRIBUTOR BIOGRAPHIES

MATTHEW BOTTIGLIERI lives in Portland, Oregon with his lovely wife, Jen, and his cats Mosley and Olive. He has enjoyed reading and writing weird tales ever since his mom handed him a King Conan comic when he was 8 years old. When he's not writing or heaving kettlebells, Matt enjoys playing jazz guitar, spending time with family and friends, and exploring Oregon.

TREY CAUSEY is an addiction psychiatrist and medical director of a residential treatment facility. He writes a blog called From the Sorcerer's Skull and has published Weird Adventures, a pulp fantasy role-playing game setting. Outside the rpg arena, he wrote the comic Planet X, a contestant in Zuda Comics' (DC Comic's webcomics imprint) November 2008 competition and Hellbent: Infamous Monsters, currently available on Graphic.Ly.

ALEX J. CHRISTY was born in the suburbs of Los Angeles to Scientologist parents, and developed a taste for the weird early on. Attracted to the works of Lovecraft, Howard, Tolkien and Leiber, he felt an immediate connection with those fantastic stories and a strong kinship with their authors. It wasn't long before he picked up pen and paper and began writing stories of his own, tales of adventure and horror that he shared with his closest friends around their weekly gaming table. Alexander lives in Los Angeles with his beautiful fiancée Lisa and their strangely intelligent orange tabby cat, Rusty. The Eye of Hytuuzsh is his first published story.

CHRISTOPHER CONKLIN (ARTIST) was raised in a quiet suburb on Long Island where he spent his days playing Dungeons & Dragons and drawing. A five-year pilgrimage North to the mountains took him from the suburbs and into the world at large. Now Chris has returned to the quiet suburbs of his early years, where by day he molds the minds the youth and by night is a co-owner a gaming store called Legendary Realms and continues to play D&D and draw.
Contact: Rauthik@aol.com
Art: http://rauthik.deviantart.com/
Business: www.legendaryrealmsgames.com

ALASDAIR CUNNINGHAM was born in Scotland and raised in KwaZulu Natal, South Africa. He writes radio theatre, background and character stories for Bushido – the game, and occasionally ventures into script writing. He is currently working on a novel and an anthology of short stories. He lives with his wife and son in Cape Town, South Africa.

GARNETT ELLIOTT lives and works in Tucson, Arizona. Most of his published work has been in the crime and pulp genres, with stories appearing in Alfred Hitchcock's Mystery Magazine, Needle, Reloaded (Both Barrels 2), Uncle B's Drive-In Fiction, Blood and Tacos, Beat to a Pulp, Battling Boxing Stories, and numerous online magazines and print anthologies. He has been writing the ongoing Drifter Detective epub series, including the most recent installment, Hell up in Houston. His fantasy-themed stories have appeared in Swords and Sorcery Magazine and the Eldritch Dark, the latter being a website devoted to Clark Ashton Smith. Mr. Elliott has also written for Chaosium, and penned a series o swords and sorcery adventures for the Barbarians of Lemuria RPG, under the name 'G-Man.' These adventures are available for free download from the Venomous Pao's RPG website, StrangeStoneshttp://www.strangestones.com/downloads/

JOSH GRABOFF holds an MA in Medieval Studies from Boston College. The tales in this volume are his first non-academic published works.

TOBIAS LOC is a writer of strange fantasy. His current project is a series of interlinking short stories that explore creation mythology, gnostic symbolism, and certain elements of the Western Mystery Tradition within a sword and sorcery setting. The story As Above is the second in this series.

Tobias is also interested in board game and role-playing game design. He is the co-founder of Blasted Tower Games and has designed two board games and one browser game. Other interests include cryptography, animation, Egyptian hieroglyphics, hermetic philosophy, and bronze casting.

JAMES MACGEORGE was exiled, five years ago, from the snow-capped mountains and rolling hills of Upstate New York, and banished to the infernal wastelands of Texas. While his diaspora has not been without its challenges, it has brought him a wife, a pool and a pickup truck. While this is his first time in print, he is an avid gamer, and is the author of the forthcoming roleplaying game, From the Ashes.

JARED PLUMBER is a disgruntled attorney who recently went from an employee in a medium-sized firm to the owner of his own small firm. He lives in the same small town near the Rocky Mountains where he was born and has spent his entire life (except for a brief period spent as a minister in Taiwan). Jared wishes on a daily basis that he could flee with his loving wife and his wonderful children (a.k.a. "the Horde") to a mountain hideaway and live there, carefree, to the end of his days. He considers his writing and gaming to be his creative haven, an emotional safe house, a metaphysical rubber room in which to vent and rant and otherwise keep from kicking the dog.

TIMOTHY P. REMP B.A. is the Assistant Editor and contributor for Shroud Magazine. He is also a member of the Horror Writers' Association (HWA), and New England Horror Writers Association (NEHW). He has had several flash and short stories published on-line, print and in several anthologies. He has been a finalist in four script writing contest and currently is judging scripts for the New Hampshire Film Festival 2013 and with be Co Director 2014.

JOSH REYNOLDS is a professional freelance writer of moderate skill and exceptional confidence. His work has appeared in anthologies such as Miskatonic River Press' Horror for the Holidays, and in periodicals such as Innsmouth Magazine and Lovecraft eZine. In addition to his own work, he has written for several tie-in franchises, including Gold Eagle's Executioner line and Black Library's Warhammer Fantasy line. Feel free to stop by his blog,http://joshuamreynolds.wordpress.com/ to check up on him or to tell him he's wrong about whatever it is you disagree with him about.

SEAN P. ROBSON is a palaeontologist with a Ph.D. in Geological Sciences from the University of Saskatchewan. When not studying the chitinous, scaled, fanged, tentacled, and multi-appendaged monstrosities that inhabited Earth's distant past, he writes dark fantasy fiction while listening to Dead Can Dance and drinking way too much coffee. He lives in Winnipeg, Manitoba with his wife, daughter, and alarmingly smelly cat.

AFTERWORD

This publication has been a labour of love born of a desire to provide a venue for the publication of weird fiction reminiscent of that published in pulp periodicals, such as Weird Tales, in the early- to mid- twentieth century. For more than thirty years I've been a fan of the weird fiction written by authors such as Robert E. Howard, H.P. Lovecraft, Clark Ashton Smith, Fritz Leiber, and many others. I was introduced to these authors, as were so many of my generation, by list of inspirational reading (Appendix N) at the back of E. Gary Gygax's Advanced Dungeons & Dragons Dungeon Master's Guide, and they left an indelible mark on my adolescent psyche that has guided my taste in speculative fiction ever since.

The title of this anthology series, Libram Mysterium was chosen to honour speculative fiction legend, Jack Vance, who passed away at the age of ninety-six, just a few weeks before Pulp Mill Press opened to submissions. The word libram was coined by Vance in his 1950 classic, The Dying Earth, and it has gained a great deal of traction among his fans and the role-playing game community as a synonym for a book of arcane lore. There could be no better title for this anthology, which is dedicated to the memory of Jack Vance and his literary legacy.

Although I had been contemplating this project for several years, it might never have gotten off the ground if Tim Shorts hadn't provided the motivation to get started. I would also like to thank Ken Harrison and Jared Plummer for their assistance in getting Pulp Mill Press rolling, especially for designing the blog and Facebook page. Most of all I would like to thank the contributors for their submissions and Chris Conklin for providing the cover and interior illustrations. This book would not have been possible without their hard work and perseverance.

Sean Robson
January, 2014

www.ingramcontent.com/pod-product-compliance
Lightning Source LLC
Chambersburg PA
CBHW060110260626
47160CB00005B/1845